"Maybe this isn't such a good idea," Kullen told her.

His voice strained as if every fiber in his being was at war with itself, with the intense desire for fulfillment.

"Why?" she whispered, afraid of what she was feeling. And even more afraid *not* to be feeling it.

"Because," he told her honestly, since this was no time for lies or half-truths, "holding you like this makes me remember how much I wanted you."

"'Wanted?'" she repeated. There was a ribbon of sorrow in her voice, as if she regretted what might have been but no longer was. Regretted a loss of something she had never been allowed to experience. "Does that mean you don't anymore?"

Kullen felt her breath gliding along his neck. Felt his gut tighten into a tight, tight knot.

He could barely breathe. She literally did take his breath away.

Kullen hardly remembered the precise moment his control shattered.

Dear Reader,

If you've been around me for any length of time, you might have noticed a pattern forming. I begin a series by setting limits for myself. Three books, four books, five books. All the series I plot have a finite number. Once I'm in the world I created, I can't say goodbye. Matchmaking Mamas was supposed to be about three lifelong best friends meddling in their daughters' lives in order to find the perfect match for them. Three friends, three daughters, ta-dum, end of story. Well, not quite. One of the friends has a son in addition to a daughter... and then, there are those handy relatives, who also need to find true love.

So, you see, I can't seem to help myself. I'm a compulsive storyteller and there's nothing I love more than a sequel. I know I should try to find a local branch of storytellers anonymous to join, and I would—if I wasn't having so much fun.

As always, I thank you for reading and with all my heart, I wish you someone to love who loves you back.

Love,

Marie Ferrarella

UNWRAPPING THE PLAYBOY

MARIE FERRARELLA

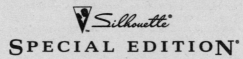

SPECIAL EDITION®

Published by Silhouette Books

America's Publisher of Contemporary Romance

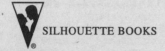 SILHOUETTE BOOKS

Recycling programs for this product may not exist in your area.

ISBN-13: 978-0-373-65566-3

UNWRAPPING THE PLAYBOY

Selected Books by Marie Ferrarella

Silhouette Special Edition

°*Mother in Training* #1785
Romancing the Teacher #1826
§§*Remodeling the Bachelor* #1845
§§*Taming the Playboy* #1856
§§*Capturing the Millionaire* #1863
°°*Falling for the M.D.* #1873
~*Diamond in the Rough* #1910
--*The Bride with No Name* #1917
~*Mistletoe and Miracles* #1941
††*Plain Jane and the Playboy* #1946
~*Travis's Appeal* #1958
§*Loving the Right Brother* #1977
The 39-Year-Old Virgin #1983
~*A Lawman for Christmas* #2006
¤¤*Prescription for Romance* #2017
¶*Doctoring the Single Dad* #2031
¶*Fixed Up with Mr. Right?* #2041
¶*Finding Happily-Ever-After* #2060
¶*Unwrapping the Playboy* #2084

°Talk of the Neighborhood
*Cavanaugh Justice
†The Doctors Pulaski
§§The Sons of Lily Moreau
°°The Wilder Family
~Kate's Boys
††The Fortunes of Texas:
    Return to Red Rock
¤¤The Baby Chase
¶Matchmaking Mamas

Silhouette Romantic Suspense

The Heart of a Ruler #1412
**The Woman Who
    Wasn't There* #1415
*Cavanaugh Watch #1431
†*Her Lawman on Call* #1451
†*Diagnosis: Danger* #1460
My Spy #1472
†*Her Sworn Protector* #1491
*Cavanaugh Heat #1499
†*A Doctor's Secret* #1503
†*Secret Agent Affair* #1511
**Protecting His Witness* #1515
Colton's Secret Service #1528
The Heiress's 2-Week Affair #1556
*Cavanaugh Pride #1571
**Becoming a Cavanaugh* #1575
The Agent's Secret Baby #1580
**The Cavanaugh Code* #1587
**In Bed with the Badge* #1596
**Cavanaugh Judgment* #1612
Colton by Marriage #1616
**Cavanaugh Reunion* #1623

MARIE FERRARELLA

This *USA TODAY* bestselling and RITA® Award-winning author has written more than two hundred books for Silhouette Books and Harlequin Books, some under the name of Marie Nicole. Her romances are beloved by fans worldwide. Visit her website at www.marieferrarella.com.

To Charlie,
who had my heart
from the moment he walked into
my second-period English class
when I was fourteen

Chapter One

"Kullen, you need a woman in your life."

Kullen Manetti smiled at his widowed mother across the small table at Vesuvius.

Not bad. This had to be a new record. Theresa Manetti had managed to go through the main course before she'd brought up the subject. His lack of a better half was, after all, one of his mother's top-ten topics whenever they spent more than a few moments in each other's company.

Since his sister, Kate, had succumbed some six months ago to the charms of one bank manager by the name of Jackson Wainwright, leaving him the last man standing and holding down the "single" fort in their small group of second-generation friends, his unwedded state had become his mother's number one favorite topic.

But his mother, bless her, had just missed one very obvious point with her comment.

"Mom, I have lots of women in my life," Kullen reminded her.

Theresa's blue eyes narrowed just a bit as she stuck to her guns. In the last year, she and her best friends, Maizie and Cecilia, had arranged successful pairings for their three stubbornly single, career-obsessed daughters. Theresa had become far more confident about her abilities and her judgment than she'd been prior to this venture.

Granted, she did run her own business and had for a number of years. But on the home front, she was the quietest and shyest of the threesome, women she'd been friends with ever since they'd met—and bonded—in the third grade.

Maizie, a self-starting real estate broker, had spearheaded what she had initially referred to as Operation: Matchmaking Mamas. Cecilia had been the one who'd backed her wholeheartedly despite veiling her enthusiasm with a bit of sarcasm. But then Cecilia had always been a tad sarcastic.

As for Theresa, her way was to cross her fingers and fervently pray. On occasion, she would say something—completely unobtrusively—about wishing she could see her son and daughter settle down. Both Kate and Kullen were lawyers at what had once been their father's topflight family law firm. For all intents and purposes, Kate had been married monastically to her work for quite some time, while Kullen, equally as sharp, had somehow managed to be successful while still systematically enjoying the company of every attractive, unattached woman in a fifty-mile radius. He had no qualms about branching to outlying areas once his immediate supply was exhausted. No relationship—if it actually could be called that—went beyond a few weeks. Six weeks was the limit and those, in Kullen's opinion, were considered to be long term, as well as exceedingly rare.

It hurt Theresa's heart that her handsome, successful, dynamic son had no desire to find that one special woman who promised to turn his world on its ear and make him want to be—please, God—monogamous.

"A *decent* woman in your life," Theresa now qualified firmly.

Beaming, Kullen leaned in closer. "Ah, well, for that I have you," he told her, brushing a quick kiss on his mother's temple. "And Kate. And, of course, those delightfully charming, probing friends of yours, Maizie and Cecilia."

His mother, he knew, got together with the latter two at least once a week to play poker—allegedly. What they did, in actuality, was strategize. Now that Kate, Nikki and Jewel were spoken for, he imagined that the women were pressed for a new project. Well, much as he loved his mother and her friends—women he had thought were his aunts for the first ten years of his life—their next project sure as hell wasn't going to be him.

Theresa drew up her small frame and sat schoolgirl straight in her chair as she scrutinized her firstborn. Kullen was tall, dark and handsome, just as his father had been. Except that Kullen's features were finer, chiseled. Almost aristocratic in appearance. That he got from her. His wandering eye, well, that was anyone's guess.

"Kullen—"

He knew that tone. Knew, too, that it was in his best interest to cut her off as quickly as possible before she built up a full head of steam. He didn't want to end this pleasant lunch on a sour note. These days, the pace of his life had picked up, especially since one of the senior partners, Ronald Simmons, had retired last month. Consequently, he didn't get the opportunity to visit with his mother as often as he liked.

All things considered, he really did enjoy his mother's company. Theresa Manetti was kind, sympathetic and giving and he loved her for it. In true selfless-mother fashion, she put her family before herself.

His father, Kullen thought and not for the first time, had been an exceedingly lucky man. Unfortunately, Anthony Manetti had been far too consumed with his work to notice just how lucky he was. From its very inception, the family law firm, then known as Manetti, Rothchild and Simmons, had been his father's life, and it wasn't until he and then Kate had joined the firm that Anthony Manetti had taken real notice of either one of them.

Kate, Kullen knew, had had it particularly hard because, on top of being a perfectionist, their late father had been a chauvinist. Until his dying day, Anthony Manetti believed that anyone of the female gender—outside of a few outstanding women in world politics—was not as mentally equipped as a man in any field. Especially the law. He demanded twice as much from Kate just to put her on equal footing with the other junior lawyers in the firm.

Too bad, Dad. You had the devotion of two good

women and you never even knew it, Kullen thought, even as he verbally headed his mother off at the pass.

"Really, Mom, I would think that you and your ladies would be far more interested in tackling your own lives, or if you must, gang up on poor, lonely Cousin Kennon."

Like his sister and her two friends, his cousin Kennon was one of those exceedingly busy career women—she had her own decorating business—who maintained that they were far too preoccupied to invest themselves in a relationship. In his opinion, Kennon was perfect for his mother's next project.

He was not.

On the contrary, he, Kullen Manetti, was having a lot of fun and absolutely none of his so-called *dalliances*—his mother's word—were serious. Which was just the way he liked it.

This way, nothing got bruised. Not his ego, not his heart.

Both had been painfully battered once before, and it was more than enough for him. But it had happened so long ago and now felt like something he'd read about in a book or seen in a movie. Not real heartbreak.

Except that it was real.

But he'd been another person then. Naive and dumb. He liked himself better now: sharp, successful, with more than enough phone numbers of eligible young women.

Theresa tilted her head ever so slightly—a habit that Kate had picked up—and repeated with a smattering of confusion, "Our own lives?"

"Yes, last time I checked, neither you, Maizie or

Cecilia were making any plans to walk down that flower-laden aisle—or even check into a hotel," he added with a mischievous, wicked wink, then asked, "Or have you been holding out on me?"

When he looked like that—especially with that grin—Kullen reminded her of Anthony the very first time she'd ever seen him, Theresa thought as a wave of affection washed over her. Back then, Anthony hadn't been so driven. Before life took over, Anthony Manetti had been romantic and fun, in addition to heart-stoppingly good-looking.

She missed both men terribly—the boyishly charming man Anthony had initially been and the dynamic, brilliant man he became. She just wished he hadn't left her out of the second phase. In retrospect, their time together had been much too short. Anthony had been—and always would be—the one true love of her life.

"No, I'm not 'holding out' on you, Kullen. Being married to your father was enough for me," Theresa told her son. "I consider myself one of the lucky ones. I *had* my happiness." She knew that Maizie and Cecilia felt the same way about their late husbands. "It's the kind of happiness I want for your sister—and for you."

There was humor in his magnetic blue eyes as Kullen replied, "Oh, I'm happy, Mom."

Her son dated women whose IQ's rivaled those of three-day-old blueberry muffins and they both knew it. Gorgeous or not, the whole lot of them were what her generation had referred to as bimbos.

"Genuinely happy," Theresa emphasized. She tried to word it tactfully. "It's the difference between gorging yourself on a box of chocolates and having something substantial to eat that's nutritious and good for you. One does nothing but give you excess, artery-clogging fat, the other makes you healthy and strong, able to live your life to the fullest."

Kullen laughed, shaking his head. "Trust you to fall back on food analogies."

While Maizie had her own real estate company and Cecilia ran a high-end cleaning service, his mother had created an enterprise from her own outstanding talent. A masterful chef, his mother owned her catering business. The woman could make a feast out of a discarded old shoe and have people begging for more.

However, he had no intentions of his mother making *anything* out of him, least of all a candidate for a blind date.

"No offense, Mom, but I'm not a meat-and-potatoes kind of guy. I've got a sweet tooth and chocolates suit my needs just fine." He looked at her with affection, knowing that she said what she did out of love and he couldn't really fault her for it. But he did have to be honest with her. "And I don't intend to change anytime soon."

Theresa was not discouraged. "Kate felt the same way."

"Kate wasn't happy," he reminded her. "I am." Long since finished with both his dessert and coffee, he moved both aside and leaned in closer to his mother. "Right now, you're batting a thousand, Mom. If you put me into the mix, you're going to see your average drop to five hundred."

Theresa sighed softly. "It's not even baseball season."

Kullen's amusement increased. He knew the effort his mother had made just to be knowledgeable about something that was near and dear to his heart, and he loved her for it. Had things turned out differently eight years ago, he might have married someone a lot like her. But then, he'd made a fatal error in judgment.

All ancient history, he reminded himself. He had since discovered that they'd broken the mold when it came to women like his mother. Another reason for him to remain a confirmed bachelor. Why enter a relationship where arguing and discontent lay in wait for him? He was far better off the way he was—free, and happy to be that way.

"It wouldn't drop to five hundred," his mother said with feeling. When he looked at her with a slightly bemused expression, she went on to say, "You're forgetting Nikki and Jewel." They were Maizie and Cecilia's daughters, both successfully paired with men who were nothing short of fantastic.

"No, I didn't forget Nikki and Jewel, and even if I did, you'd be here to remind me." He had no intention of going around and around about this. "Go out a winner, Mom," he advised. "It's always the best way. That's why the *Seinfeld* cast called it quits after nine seasons. They knew that it was nice to go out on top."

That could *not* win her over. Theresa pressed her lips together, wishing that Kullen would listen to reason. Worrying that something would go wrong in the *very* near future.

"This isn't a TV comedy series," she told him. "It's your life."

"Yes," he agreed pointedly, "it is." It was his life

and he wasn't about to allow it to get railroaded just to satisfy his mother's dreams and the machinations of her two friends. "And I'm not twelve years old anymore," he reminded her. At thirty he had long since become his own man.

"If you were," Theresa folded her hands before her on the table, "we wouldn't be having this conversation. I know enough about the law to know that it's illegal to get married at twelve—in *any* state."

"We're not having this conversation," Kullen said with a touch of humor as he rose to his feet. The check had been paid between dessert and coffee. "And I've got to be getting back to the office." Kullen bent over and kissed her lightly. The faint scent of jasmine, his mother's favorite fragrance, greeted him. "Got a full schedule laid out for this afternoon."

Theresa suppressed a smile. She knew all about his full schedule for this afternoon. Knew something about it that he didn't. Composing herself, she allowed a smile to enter her voice as she murmured, "My son, the successful lawyer."

He paused for a moment. If he didn't know better, he would have said she was scheming. "You know, Mom, for some mothers that would be more than enough."

She couldn't resist answering him on this point. Someday, she mused, he would put all the pieces together. But right now, they would have to remain "pieces" just a tiny bit longer. "I'm not 'some' mother, Kullen. I'm *your* mother." He looked at her quizzically. She went a step further. "And as your mother—"

"You have been delightful company," he told her, cutting in before the conversation made yet another

U-turn to the subject of his dating. "'Bye. I've really gotta go."

And with that, he began to make his retreat. But her voice stopped him.

"Kullen—"

Something in his mother's voice caught his attention. He turned around and waited. "Yes?"

Because she was an honest woman, Theresa felt compelled to be up-front with her son. In this case, that would entail telling him that last weekend she had catered a rather large charity luncheon for Anne McCall, Lilli McCall's mother. The conversation got around to their children. When Anne had told her that her daughter was back in Bedford and, coincidentally, was in dire need of a good family lawyer, Theresa's heart had begun to race.

More than anything, Theresa wanted to tell her son that she'd been quick to mention he had become a lawyer and that she'd given his number to a greatly relieved Anne. She very much wanted to tell him that this afternoon he would be seeing Lilli, a woman, she'd discovered quite by accident, that he'd dated briefly in law school.

But because Theresa knew that he would see this as a setup on her part and thus would most likely palm the whole case off on Kate, Theresa forced a smile and merely told him, "Have a nice afternoon, dear."

Returning her smile, he said, "Thanks, I will." And then, her six-foot-two, dark-haired, handsome son went off, utterly unsuspecting, to start his afternoon.

And just possibly, Theresa fervently hoped, to begin the rest of his life.

* * *

Lilli McCall wasn't sure that this was such a good idea.

Before leaving the house, she'd picked up the phone three times to call Kullen's office to cancel her appointment. But each time she began to press the numbers she stopped. If she broke this appointment, she would have to find another lawyer. And find one in a hurry.

Time was running out on her. She couldn't just close her eyes and pretend that everything was all right—because it so wasn't. It hadn't been all right since she'd opened Elizabeth Dalton's registered letter several weeks ago, completely out of the blue. The letter that had made her move back to Bedford in hopes of eluding the woman. She should have known better. The woman had tentacles that reached everywhere.

A second letter had found her here.

The letter, written on fine linen, dripped with condescension and sarcasm. Worse, it had contained a threat that even a seven-year-old couldn't miss.

A threat that she wouldn't allow to happen. She intended to fight Elizabeth Dalton with her dying breath, if it came to that.

But that meant going to court—or at least getting a damn good lawyer who would not just fight the good fight for her, but win.

Win by any means possible.

If she could fight a clean fight, she would, but she wasn't so naive she believed for one moment that Elizabeth Dalton intended to fight fairly. The widow of a man who had been heir to a pharmaceutical empire, she detested people who opposed her and loved getting her way.

Loved winning.

Lilli had no doubt that the rich socialite would instruct her lawyer to use every dirty trick in the book to get what she wanted.

And what the woman wanted was her son.

Elizabeth's grandson.

The problem was that she didn't know any lawyers, good *or* bad. Why should she? Despite three quarters of a year of law school behind her, she'd never needed one before, never knew anyone who'd needed one before, which now left her at a terrible disadvantage.

But she knew Kullen. Knew that he was good and kind and caring, so that was a start. Because he had turned out to be a lawyer and was still right here in Bedford, maybe fate was finally being kind to her.

Still, arriving ten minutes early for her appointment, Lilli sat in her small, tidy blue car in Rothchild, McDowell and Simmons's parking lot, debating one last time the wisdom of what she was about to do. Debating, again, canceling her appointment.

She'd even pushed his office number on her keypad, her finger hovering over the send button, before she flipped her phone closed, shoved it into her purse and then got out of the car. She all but marched into the six-story building. But when she stepped into the elevator, Lilli felt not unlike a doomed soul walking the last mile. Or riding up to it, as it were.

Jonathan, think of Jonathan, she told herself. *Jonathan is all that matters. You have to keep him out of that woman's clutches. Or she'll turn him into a carbon copy of his father.*

And that, Lilli knew, would be a fate worse than death.

The elevator door opened all too quickly and she got out.

As she walked the short distance to the impressive offices of Rothchild, McDowell and Simmons, Lilli fervently prayed she was doing the right thing.

Because she was putting her son's future—and his fate—into the hands of a man she'd walked out on all those years ago.

Chapter Two

There were days, Kullen thought, when life seemed like a reenactment of the Indianapolis 500. But instead of cars, the minutes and hours madly whizzed by him. It was all he could do to keep things remotely straight.

If he were honest, he doubted he could keep his sanity if it wasn't for the woman his father had hired as his chief secretary so many years ago.

Selma Walker was no longer a secretary. These days, she was an administrative assistant, a title that seemed to annoy her at times, or "vex" her, as she was wont to say. She liked "calling a rose a rose," and she was a secretary. A damn good secretary. And proud of it.

Selma was only slightly less old than the proverbial hills. A small, thin bit of a woman with unnaturally black hair, she was, despite her steamroller attitude and undisclosed age, sharp as a tack. It was Selma who kept Kullen's—as well as everyone else's—schedule straight. She personally filled in appointments on his desk calendar as well as, reluctantly, his computer. She really distrusted anything electronic and this included the elevator. Every morning and evening, she took the stairs.

The woman had told him more than once that she liked the feel of pen and paper and that, come a power failure—or a sunspot—everything electronic would be rendered useless. At that point, all the old-fashioned methods, heavily relying on brain power, would be called into service because the traditional methods, she maintained, were the best.

If Selma had an actual failing, other than her less than sunny disposition, it was her handwriting. Surprisingly for one of her generation, it was far worse than chicken scratch. When this was pointed out, she took umbrage, tersely saying that she could read every word. This placed her in a very small group that numbered exactly one.

Which was why, although he'd glanced at his desk calendar, Kullen wound up caught completely off guard when he heard the knock on his door and instructed the person on the other side, his new client, to come in.

Up until that point, all he'd known about the new client was that she was female and single. He'd learned to recognize what in Selma's handwriting passed for either "Mrs." or "Mr." The former had one scribbled letter more. The third title, Ms., Selma refused to acknowledge or insert. To her, unmarried women were Miss, not Ms. She insisted that Ms. was an abbreviation for manuscript and wouldn't attach it to a human being. Thus, the name he'd fleetingly looked at had no title before it.

While the client's actual name was a mystery to him, Kullen saw no reason for concern. The name of this single female would inevitably come out during the introductions. He'd long since given up verbally dueling with Selma over her handwriting, preferring to have his wits challenged by his new client rather than his stubborn administrative assistant.

Knowing his new client's gender and general marital status left Kullen entirely unprepared for the actual sight of that same new client when she entered.

Eight years had passed but he would have known her anywhere.

Lilli.

For the longest time, Lilli's delicate, almost waif-like image had been stitched on his heart and even now, although shut away, it still occupied a small, darkened corner of his soul.

Surprise, joy and anger swirled around within Kullen. Along with deep confusion. Why was she here?

It took him a second to remember that regular breathing was essential to keep from keeling over, head first, onto his desk, and that he'd stopped breathing the moment he'd seen her enter.

Rising to his feet, Kullen felt as if his body didn't quite belong to him. Felt, instead, as if this was a small segment of a recurring dream that still, on occasion, haunted him. Breaking up into tiny fragments once he was fully awake.

But he was awake now.

Wasn't he?

"Lilli?" he whispered uncertainly.

Part of him expected the client to eye him quizzically,

not recognizing the name because there was no earthly reason for this to be the woman who had bolted out of his life the night after he'd produced an engagement ring and asked her to marry him. Not only bolted, but disappeared without a trace. No one knew where she'd gone or why she'd suddenly dropped out of law school—and, for all intents and purposes, out of life.

But this *was* Lilli standing before him. Kullen would have bet his soul on it.

The next moment, as a small, incredibly sad smile curved her lips, his silent wager was validated and he held on to his soul a little longer.

"Hello, Kullen." The slender blonde he'd once envisioned spending the rest of his life with stood behind the black leather, ergonomically correct chair that faced his desk, making no move to claim it. "May I sit?" she asked him in a soft, melodic voice that seemed to drift to him on an invisible cloud.

He felt as if he'd just been struck dumb. It took another long moment for him to engage his brain properly, to clamp down on the cauldron of emotions still bubbling up.

"Yes. Sit. Please." All things considered, he was surprised his tongue still worked.

Kullen gestured toward the soft leather chair. Belatedly, he slowly sank into his own. It amazed him how, despite her rather diminutive size, Lilli seemed to fill up the room with her presence.

He couldn't take his eyes off her, a very small part of him still fully expecting her to disappear because his mind was playing a terrible trick on him.

But it wasn't playing a trick. Taking a deep breath,

he went on automatic pilot, saying things he'd said to other clients scores of times before. Doing his best to shake off this surreal feeling that held him captive.

"Can I offer you something to drink?" he asked, nodding toward the narrow black-lacquered side table, where various necessities of life stood at the ready. "Coffee? Tea? Bottled water?"

She shook her head with each choice. "No, thank you. I'm not thirsty."

He nodded, rigidly taking his seat again. "All right then, maybe you'll tell me what you are," he suggested tersely.

Kullen caught himself before he went any further. With effort, he banked down the bitterness swelling in his chest and crowding his throat. He squared his shoulders ever so imperceptively and asked the only logical question.

"What are you doing here, Lilli?"

She cut to the heart of it, because she knew he had every right to turn her away.

If he did that, she didn't know what she would do.

Start over again, the way you did the last time.

In the years since she'd abruptly left him, Lilli had discovered that she was stronger than she'd ever believed. It was amazing how someone small and helpless depending on her could transform her. She was a survivor now.

"I'm here to ask for your help," she said.

The simple words seemed to pierce his chest.

Kullen wanted to know what gave her the right to surface now, after all this time. What gave her the utter gall to ask him for his help?

Eight years ago he would have done anything for her. All she had to do then was to ask. He would have been willing to literally give up his life for her. She had to have known that. But even so, she had all but spit in his face. And left.

The seconds stretched out into a minute as he sat, looking at her. Studying her. Finally, in a deceptively calm voice, he asked, "So all the other men in the world are dead?"

She stared at him, confused. The question made no sense. "Excuse me?"

"That was the way you made me feel when you took off, that you wouldn't have anything to do with me even if I was the last man on earth. Since you're here, I'm assuming that for some reason, all the other men in the world have been mysteriously terminated, although I have to say I don't see how that's possible, since I passed a few of them in the hall not fifteen minutes ago." He lifted his shoulders in a casual, dismissive shrug. "I guess I must have missed the Armageddon that took place in the last ten minutes." He leaned forward over his desk, his voice lowering to a rumble. "Or did it happen in less?"

Lilli recoiled emotionally despite sitting ramrod straight.

She knew she had that coming. That and probably more. Lost in her own predicament, she'd treated him shamefully.

Lilli took a breath. She should have known better than to come. Though Kullen had every right to be angry at her, even to hate her, hearing his cold, emotionless voice as he addressed her hurt far too much for her to withstand.

Hurt, because even with everything that had happened, everything that she'd done, she knew in her heart that Kullen Manetti was the only man who had ever mattered to her. The only man who *would* ever matter to her.

The only man she'd ever loved—even if she had put him through hell. And he was better looking than ever. Then he'd been almost pretty. Maturity had found him and now he was breathtakingly handsome. She felt the attraction immediately. Just as she had all those years ago.

"This was a mistake," she told him stiffly. Pushing against the floor, she moved back her chair. "I shouldn't have come." As she rose to her feet, she told him, "I didn't mean to bother you."

Logically, Kullen knew he should just let her walk out. It had taken him a long time, but he had managed to successfully reinvent himself, to become a different man. He didn't want to go back to that place where feelings had such overwhelming power over him. That place where he'd ached so badly he didn't think he could survive the night without the woman he loved.

He needed to remember that, remember the price he'd paid for letting down his guard.

For loving her.

The pep talk wasn't working. He could feel himself weakening. Slipping.

Despite his resolve, something in those light blue eyes of hers spoke to him, pulled at him, just the way it had that first time so many years ago.

"What was a mistake," he told Lilli crisply, struggling with the insane urge to take her into his arms and just hold her, "was your disappearing on me eight years ago."

On the verge of leaving his office, Lilli stopped just shy of the door. She didn't turn around. Her voice was flat as she addressed her words to the beveled glass. "I had my reasons."

"Which you didn't think enough of me to share," he pointed out. He never meant to say this out loud, but the question tumbled out anyway. "Did you really hate me that much?"

Stunned, Lilli swung around to face him. "Hate you?" she echoed incredulously. "I didn't hate you. I didn't want to hurt you."

"And that's why you ripped out my heart and threw it down the garbage disposal? So you wouldn't hurt me?" he demanded. "C'mon, Lilli, you can do better than that."

She closed her eyes for a moment, trying to seal away the tears that had suddenly welled up. "You don't understand," Lilli whispered.

It wasn't easy to hold his ground, not when everything inside him, despite all that had gone down, just wanted to comfort her. To hold her and remember what life had once been like.

Only self-preservation managed to hold him in check. "Then explain it to me."

But she just shook her head. There was too much ground to cover. And too much time had passed. Had life not scarred her before he had come on the scene,

Kullen would have been perfect for her. For the Lilli she'd once been.

Before.

Lilli shook her head again. "It's complicated. I can't…" Her voice threatened to break. "I've got to go." Her hand went to the doorknob.

Kullen cut the distance between them in strides he didn't remember taking. One moment he was across the room, the next, he was beside her. Closing the door with the flat of his hand, he became a physical obstacle that prevented her escape.

"Why did you come?" he asked, just barely taking the edge out of his voice. "What is it you need help with?"

Maybe things would be all right after all. Maybe coming here *wasn't* a mistake. Lilli pressed her lips together as she raised her eyes to his. "I need help to save my son."

His breath left him.

Kullen felt as if he'd actually been sucker punched in the gut. For a second, he allowed the words to sink in.

"You have a son?"

He could remember that when they'd been together those few short, glorious months, in the beginning she'd all but shrank away from his touch. The first time that had happened, he'd been more puzzled than offended. Challenged, charmed by her, he worked hard to gain her trust. And he'd taken her at her word when she'd told him that she wanted to go slow. He'd thought she was one of those rare girls who was serious about "saving herself" for the right man. Saving herself for her husband.

He'd been so crazy about her, he would have gone along with anything she'd said as long as it meant that she'd remain in his life. That eventually, she would marry him and be his.

He supposed that made him incredibly naive and stupid, in light of the situation—as well as what she'd told him just now. She hadn't been saving herself; she'd just been keeping herself from him.

"Yes," Lilli replied quietly. "I have a son." *And I'll do anything to save him. Anything.*

Kullen glanced down at her left hand. There was no ring on it. No ring and no faint, pale lines to indicate that there once had been. Had everything she'd once told him been a lie?

"What about a husband?" he asked her evenly. "He around anywhere?"

She raised her chin and her eyes met his. "I don't have one."

"Divorced?" he guessed. His temper started to flare. "Widowed? How about just separated from a significant other? Got one of those around?"

"No. No. No." Lilli answered each question in turn.

Then, apparently, there was only one conclusion to be reached. The words were on his lips before he could think to stop himself. "Did I miss the announcement of another Immaculate Conception?"

The moment he said it, he saw the walls literally go up. He read her body language and blocked her as she reached for the door again. His anger had gotten the best of him. What he'd just said was beneath him, and he knew it.

"All right, I'm sorry," he apologized. "But I did feel I

had a right to say that." The walls around her remained up. "When we were together," he reminded her, "you said you were saving yourself."

"I never actually said that in so many words," Lilli pointed out. She hadn't said those words because, through no fault of her own, they wouldn't have been true. She'd let him believe what he wanted because the truth had been too painful for her to face.

Even now it was difficult.

His eyes narrowed. "Then I was just some idiot you were laughing at?"

"No!" she protested with feeling. "You were sweet and kind and sensitive—"

His scowl deepened. "In other words, an idiot," he said.

She shook her head with feeling. "No, not an idiot, a hero." Her eyes held his. He saw the passion within them as she told him, "You saved me."

He had no recollection of any heroic act on his part, other than exercising an almost superhuman effort to restrain his raging hormones and abide by her wishes even though, more than anything on earth, he longed to be intimate with her.

"Saved you?" he echoed.

Lilli nodded. "If you hadn't been so patient with me, so kind, if you hadn't gone out of your way to *be* there for me," she underscored, "I would have killed myself." And she meant it. She'd been completely hopeless, and he'd given her hope.

I would have killed myself.

It was a phrase tossed around easily, especially by younger people. He was all ready to discount it, but he saw the look in her eyes. Young, talented, smart, she had everything to live for, but she was obviously dead serious.

"Why?"

She shook her head again. "I don't want to go into that, Kullen," she told him solemnly, then drew herself up to her short stature. "I'm sorry I wasted your time like this. Send me the bill for this appointment and I'll reimburse you. It's the least I can do."

No, the least she could do was explain herself, but he knew better than to press her. Instead, as Lilli reached for the doorknob a third time, he asked, "Where are you going?"

"I have to find a lawyer."

"I'm a lawyer," he reminded her. "What's wrong with me?"

"Nothing. But I thought that you don't want to take my case—"

Kullen had no idea what he would do next or how any of this would turn out. Despite everything, he didn't want to see her walk out that door.

"I didn't say that. I don't even know what your case is," he reminded her. "What, exactly, *is* your case?"

She put it into terms as succinctly as she could. "It's a custody battle."

"Then there is a father," he concluded. And whoever the man was, he wanted custody of the child they'd had together.

"No, there's a grandmother."

Saying the words, she caught herself almost smiling. The flamboyant Elizabeth Dalton would have balked at the label, telling whoever called her a grandmother what he could do with the label and where he could put it. In the eyes of the press, Elizabeth Dalton strove to be seen as an ageless, benevolent goddess of timeless beauty. Her image, her reputation, were all-important to her.

Lilli had no doubts that if Elizabeth won custody of Jonathan, her well-adjusted little boy would be a emotional wreck in a matter of months. Perhaps sooner. All she had to do was remember the way Elizabeth's son had turned out. And what he did. It put cold fear into Lilli's heart.

"Your mother?" Kullen guessed.

"No, Elizabeth Dalton," she told him.

The mention of the high-profile socialite threw him for a moment. "The widow of the pharmaceutical heir?" he questioned. Lilli nodded. "What does she have to do with it?" he asked.

"She's the one who wants custody of my son." Lilli took a deep breath, as if trying to protect herself from the words she was saying. "And she's already told me in no uncertain terms that she will stop at nothing to get it."

Chapter Three

Like a traffic cop, Kullen held up his hand, stopping her before she went off in another direction.

"Back up. Why does Elizabeth Dalton want your son?" The flamboyant socialite took to the spotlight like the proverbial moth to the flame, but this sounded a little bizarre even for her. "Exactly what right does she have to him?"

As he waited for an explanation, he watched the wariness entering Lilli's eyes. How many times had he seen that before? Eight years ago it had taken him weeks to get her to trust him, to realize that all he wanted was for her to be happy.

She pressed her lips together before saying, "I'd rather not go into all the details right now."

There were those damn walls again. Isolating her. Keeping him out.

But this time it was different. This time it wasn't

personal. She'd sought him out in his professional capacity. She wanted his help as a lawyer, and as such he needed to establish some ground rules for them.

"If I'm going to be any use at all to you, Lilli," he said, cupping her elbow and ever so subtly guiding her back to his desk, "I'm going to have to know everything." He pulled out the chair for her but Lilli remained standing, in silent, stubborn defiance of his request. "Any lawyer will need all the details in order to properly represent you and your case."

Her case.

That made it sound so austere, so clinical. It wasn't a case, she silently insisted. It was a boy. A beautiful, sweet-tempered, innocent, blond-haired little boy. A little boy who was her reason for getting up in the morning, for her very existence. And she would die to protect him, to keep him safe and out of Elizabeth Dalton's clutches.

Lilli was still silent. Kullen sighed, attempting another approach. He sat down. "All right, I'll fill in the blanks. Stop me if I'm wrong. Elizabeth's son is the boy's father."

He paused a moment for her to contradict him, even though he was certain that, given the circumstances, she couldn't. Lilli sat down, but the uncomfortable silence continued.

"And now, out of the blue," Kullen went on, "he and his mother want custody of the boy."

Lilli looked down at her hands. "Not 'he,' just his mother," she corrected woodenly.

Kullen went with the tide. "Okay, so the boy's father doesn't want him—"

"His father *didn't* want him," she said tersely, changing the tense that he'd used.

Kullen paused. "Did something happen to make Dalton change his mind?"

"No," Lilli answered. Her voice sounded hollow to her own ears, stripped of emotion. It was the only way, even after all this time, that she could bring herself to talk about the man who had so savagely changed her life. "He's dead."

The moment she mentioned Dalton's death, Kullen vaguely recalled hearing a sound bite on the news one evening summarizing Erik Dalton's shallow life. If he remembered correctly, that was about six months ago. Thinking, he tried to summon up the details of the incident.

"It was a skiing accident, wasn't it?" he asked.

Lilli shook her head. "Boating," she corrected, then added, "From what I heard, he liked people thinking of him as some kind of a daredevil." She used the impersonal pronoun *he,* unable to make herself even say Erik Dalton's name.

Kullen continued studying her. There was so much she wasn't saying, he thought. "And that daredevil image didn't include being a father," he guessed.

Lilli could feel hateful, disparaging words rising to her lips. She'd never hated anyone, but she hated Erik Dalton with the last fiber of her being. But she had always been a truthful person and, in all fairness, in this particular situation Dalton didn't technically deserve to be called a self-centered scum.

She shrugged, trying to seem indifferent. "I never gave him the chance to turn that role down."

Damn it, Lilli, I loved you. I would have put the world at your feet if you'd married me. Was this why you left? To run into this soulless jerk's Armani-covered arms?

Kullen struggled to keep the anger out of his voice but he couldn't help asking, "Exactly what was it that you *did* give him?"

Here come the tears again, she thought, fighting to will them back. Despite her mental pep talk to the contrary, she felt terribly vulnerable and exposed. She didn't know why she felt that way, but she did.

Maybe it had to do with seeing Kullen after all these years.

Even so, Lilli absolutely refused to allow herself to cry, refused to come across as some helpless little waif, the hapless victim of a spoiled, overly privileged, rich narcissist who thought he was entitled to everything and anything he wanted.

"A note," she replied. "I wrote him a note when Jonathan was born, telling him that I thought he had a right to know that he had a son. I also told him that I didn't want anything from him. I intended to raise Jonathan on my own."

She couldn't read Kullen's expression and waited for him to say something.

When he finally spoke, it wasn't what she expected to hear. "That was rather foolish, don't you think?" he asked. "By having nothing to do with Dalton, you were denying your son a life of privilege."

His assumption made her angry. "No," she contradicted firmly, "I was protecting my son and giving him a life filled with love." She fisted her hands in her lap.

"I want Jonathan to be someone, to make something of himself and give a little back to the world. I want his life to count," she told him with passion. "I *didn't* want him to learn how to use people, how to treat them all as if they were beneath him."

His eyes never left hers. "Still, Jonathan could have had every need seen to. He can *still* have that," he pointed out.

Lilli watched him for a moment, heartsick and disappointed. Who *was* this person? The Kullen Manetti she remembered had a nobility about him. During one of their study sessions, he'd confided that he wanted to fight for the underdog. His father expected him to join *his* firm, but the thought of doing that left him feeling empty. After graduation he intended to go to work for a nonprofit organization, helping people who had nowhere else to turn.

Obviously somewhere along the line, he'd changed. He still looked like Kullen, but he no longer was that man.

Gripping the armrests on either side of her, Lilli pushed herself up to her feet again. "I guess you're not the one to help me after all." She steeled herself. "Sorry I wasted your time."

"You're repeating yourself," he told her mildly. "I'll be the one who tells you if my time's being wasted." She looked at him, perplexed. "Right now, I'm just playing devil's advocate," he continued.

"I don't need a devil's advocate," she informed him tersely. "If anything, I need an angel, because I am up against the devil in this. Elizabeth Dalton has a battalion of razor-sharp lawyers on her side." She might as well be up-front with him. "I can't afford a battalion of lawyers."

"I'm guessing," he said kindly, "that you don't have the kind of money it takes to hire one lawyer."

She wanted to protest his assumption, but couldn't. He was right and there was no point in pretending otherwise. Squaring her shoulders, she avoided looking into his eyes. If she saw pity there, it would destroy her. "I was hoping that I could pay the bill in installments."

Kullen took no delight in watching her squirm, physically or mentally. "The firm takes a few cases pro bono—"

Her head shot up. "I'm not asking for charity," she informed him, offended by the suggestion.

He knew he had to tread lightly in order not to crush her self-esteem—or insult her. "Nobody says you were. It's up to our accountant to decide whether or not taking a certain case is the right thing to do. Doing a pro bono case helps with the tax forms," he quickly interjected to keep her from protesting again. "It makes us look good. And from what I hear, the firm hasn't taken on a pro bono case this year. When you come right down to it, you might actually be doing us a favor," he told her.

Lilli sincerely doubted that. But she was desperate and she did need someone with legal expertise in her corner. She had no time to waltz around semantics. She needed to engage a lawyer soon if she had any hope of keeping her son.

So for now, she played along and pretended that she believed this fabricated story of his. "All right, if you put it that way—"

He smiled. "I do."

She had to remember not to look at him when he smiled like that. Otherwise, she ran the risk of melting right in front of him. That mischievous, boyish smile of his always got to her, managed to get through her armor. He'd won her heart with that smile.

If only things could have been different….

But they weren't, she reminded herself firmly. She had to deal in reality, not fantasies. The reality was that Elizabeth Dalton wanted to take her son away from her—and would, unless Lilli could fight her off. She felt like David, facing Goliath, and she needed a lot more than a slingshot and some rocks. She needed Kullen.

"Okay." Releasing her grip on the armrests, Lilli sank down into the chair again. But she was still far from relaxed. Until this ordeal was over, she doubted she would ever relax again. "What do you need from me?" she asked, ready to tell Kullen as much as she was able.

So many things I can't even begin to enumerate them. "To begin with, I'm going to need the boy's birth certificate," he told her.

It didn't take a rocket scientist to guess why Kullen wanted to see it. He wanted to see the name in black-and-white. "I left the space blank."

So, she hadn't lost the ability to read his mind. "You didn't list the boy's father?"

Lilli shook her head. "No."

Was she ashamed to put the man's name down? Or had the pharmaceutical heir threatened her with something to make her leave the space blank?

"Why?"

Why did Kullen have to dig like this? Her reasons

didn't matter. The only thing that mattered was that Dalton's mother wanted to take Jonathan away.

But because Kullen was waiting and wanted an answer, she gave him one.

"I wanted nothing to do with Erik Dalton. Besides, Jonathan might have Dalton DNA, but he was—and is—*my* son. *I* loved him, *I* wanted him. And I was going to make a home for him. And that's what I have been doing for the last seven years."

"Any idea why Mrs. Dalton is suddenly suing for custody after seven years? Did you get in contact with her?" He watched her expression to see her reaction as he asked the question.

"To tell her how sorry I was for her loss?" Lilli guessed. "No, I didn't." She realized that Kullen might have thought she had done it for another reason. "To tell her that she had a grandson? Again, no."

He wasn't ready to lay this line of questioning to rest yet. "Did you send photographs to her son while he was alive, showing your son's progress?"

"No. After I sent him the note telling him that he had a son I never wrote or had any contact with him again."

He studied her carefully. Would he be able to tell if she was lying to him? He was no longer sure. "Then he never wrote back or tried to get in contact with you later on?"

"No," she said with feeling. "He could have cared less about being a father. If anything, I'm sure he was relieved that I didn't want him in Jonathan's life in any manner, shape or form."

But that left a very loose end. Leaning back in his

chair, Kullen continued to study her as he asked, "Then how do you explain how Mrs. Dalton found out about Jonathan?" He gave her a way out. "Or don't you know?"

Lilli laughed shortly. "Oh, I know. She said she was going through Erik's things about a month after the funeral and she found my note telling him about the baby."

"So he kept the note."

He made it sound as if that proved there was some sentiment involved. Erik Dalton hadn't had a good bone in his body. If there had been one, it would have fled, horrified. "If he consciously kept the note, it was probably to use as a bargaining chip at some future date in case he needed it."

"Bargaining chip?" Kullen repeated. "Who would he be bargaining with?"

That was easy. "His mother. Seems she's very big on continuing the family line."

Now it was making sense. "And now that her only son is gone, she's set her sights on her grandson." It wasn't a guess.

Lilli sighed as she pressed her lips together. "That's about it."

Since he'd got her talking, he pressed his advantage. The more information he had, the better he could serve her. "What happened after she found the note?" he asked.

The events were indelibly etched on her brain. And she would forever regret taking pity on the woman. Her mistake had been to put herself in the woman's place and feel sorry for her.

"Mrs. Dalton called and asked if she could see

Jonathan. She wanted me to bring him to the house so that she could meet him."

He knew the answer before he asked, but he asked anyway. "And did you?"

Hindsight was completely useless—because there was no going back to rectify things. "In light of what she'd just been through, I thought turning her down would have been unnecessarily cruel."

Lilli McCall really was too good to be true, Kullen thought. *Careful, she ran out on you once—and obviously straight into the arms of her rich lover. Being played for a fool once is more than enough.*

"So you went to see her with Jonathan," he concluded for her.

Lilli suppressed the sigh that rose to her lips. Sighing wasn't going to help, either. She had to *do* something, get aggressive and fight this woman on her own terms. "So I went with Jonathan."

He'd started making notes to keep the events in their proper chronology. "And then what?"

"At first she seemed very nice. Her eyes literally lit up when she saw Jonathan. She said it was uncanny how much he looked like her own son at that age. That seeing Jonathan took her back, made her remember the past." Lilli's mouth hardened. "And then she talked about what she could do for Jonathan, how different his life would be if he lived with her. She started making plans as if I wasn't even standing in the room. That's when I panicked," she confessed.

He didn't blame her. Elizabeth Dalton was a statuesque, imposing woman who, he'd heard, enjoyed intimidating people. "How did the visit end?"

"Not well. Elizabeth asked me to leave Jonathan with her. I said no." She lifted one shoulder in a semi-shrug. "She doesn't like hearing that word."

He just bet she didn't. It probably surprised the hell out of her when someone as soft-spoken as Lilli stood up to her.

"She's undoubtedly not used to hearing it," he said. "So what happened after that?"

"The next afternoon, one of her lawyers got in contact with me. A very prim and proper little man who offered me money in exchange for giving up custody of my son. Offering me money," she repeated with disgust. "As if Jonathan was some kind of a toy or inanimate commodity that was for sale." Impassioned, her voice rose with each word. "Elizabeth Dalton ruined her son, I'm not going to let her ruin mine."

He made a few more notes on the page, then turned to a fresh one. "I guess they're right," he observed.

"About what?" she wanted to know.

"That no good deed goes unpunished."

"Do you think that if I hadn't taken Jonathan over to meet her—?"

He cut her short by shaking his head. He put her mind at rest. This was not her fault. None of it. "Even if you hadn't taken your son to meet his grandmother, I have a feeling the outcome would have been the same once she found out about Jonathan. And you're right in your assessment. Elizabeth Dalton likes to pride herself on getting whatever she sets her mind to."

Lilli could feel her stomach growing queasy. "Should I be worried?"

He gauged his answer slowly. "If you're asking me if

you should be getting your passports ready in order to flee the country, no. There's no need to resort to drastic measures." He took a guess at her next question and answered it before she could ask. "Do I think winning is going to be a piece of cake? No, I don't. In general, a mother's rights trump anything else that might be raised in a court of law."

"In general," she echoed. "But in this case?"

He wished he could tell her she had nothing to worry about. But he couldn't, and she needed to be prepared. "In this case, Elizabeth Dalton has a lot of powerful friends. If she and her squadron of lawyers decide to win by fair means or foul, I want you to realize we're going to have one hell of a fight on our hands."

There was only one thing that she wanted to know. "Will we win?"

He didn't deal in rainbows and fairy dust. He knew he should be prudent and cautiously tell her to be prepared for anything, because in this case they were up against a force of nature. A force of nature who numbered more than one judge in her inner circle of influential friends.

But he knew Lilli didn't need cautious words. She needed hope. He couldn't take that from her, couldn't just dash any shred of hope she might have against the rocks of reality. No matter how much she'd hurt him, he couldn't bring himself to be cruel to her.

So he gave her the most confident smile he had in his arsenal and nodded.

"Yes, Virginia," he said, paraphrasing the famous line in the legendary Christmas story, "we're going to win. It's not going to be easy, or quick," he predicted, "but we *are* going to win."

Overwhelmed, Lilli hadn't realized until just this moment how close she was to a complete meltdown. She was only a hair's breadth away. The sense of relief, of hope, was huge. This time, she allowed the tears to flow. They slid fast and furiously down her cheeks, and registered in direct contrast to the smile that curved her lips.

"Thank you," she cried, looking at him through eyes that had all but completely welled up. "Thank you."

"Don't thank me yet," he warned her. "You can save that for when the case is finally over and we walk out of the courthouse victorious."

She knew he was right. That this was far too early in the game to allow her emotions to get the better of her. Knew that they had a hard and very possibly long fight ahead of them.

But she couldn't help herself. She'd felt alone and isolated for far too long.

And she had missed him.

In one unguarded moment, Lilli let her feelings bubble up and get the better of her. She threw her arms around his neck.

"Thank you," she cried again, burying her face against his shoulder.

He felt her breath along his neck.

His stomach tightened in anticipation.

Chapter Four

Old feelings came rushing back to Kullen with the speed and intensity of a runaway freight train barreling down a steep mountain path. The urge to close his arms around Lilli, to kiss her with all his bottled-up passion nearly overwhelmed him.

It would be so easy to give in, to let his guard down just for the smallest moment and permit desire to take over.

But he knew he couldn't let himself do that.

He'd been through this before and was well aware of just how the story had ended. There was absolutely no way he would allow himself to be ripped apart again. Once was more than enough.

Once was a case of being blindsided. Twice would have meant that he was either an idiot—or a masochist. And he was neither. Moreover, he intended to remain that way. So although his heart was racing now, calling him seven kinds of a fool for not taking advantage of this opportunity shimmering before him, Kullen kept his arms rigidly at his side.

Embarrassed, feeling both self-conscious and extremely awkward, Lilli withdrew her arms and took a step back. Kullen all but radiated coldness. She succeeded in maintaining a smile on her lips, although how she was doing so was a mystery to her.

"Sorry," she murmured. "I guess I got a little overwhelmed for a second. It won't happen again."

"Nothing to be sorry about," he told her, doing his best to sound natural. Doing his best not to demand why she'd left him the way she had and then run headlong into an intimate relationship with someone else.

Someone who he *knew* couldn't have loved her half as much as he had.

Kullen took a breath, then said, "Stop at Selma's desk and ask her to give you a list of documents I'm going to need to see for this case. It's a standard list," he explained before she could ask how the administrative assistant would know what to give her. "Just tell her it's a custody dispute."

Dispute. What a civilized word for what was about to take place, Lilli thought.

"Selma's the woman at the front desk?" she asked just to be certain.

Kullen nodded. "Can't miss her. She looks like the last living cast member from the set of *The Wizard of Oz,*" he said tactfully.

It was an apt description of the woman, Lilli thought as she turned toward the door. The administrative assistant did look a great deal like an aged Munchkin. "When do you want to see me again?" she asked Kullen.

I never stopped wanting to see you, he told her silently. With effort, he forced himself to focus on more neutral terrain. He should only think of her in light of the actual business they had with one another. Nothing more.

Turning the calendar on his desk toward him, Kullen glanced at several consecutive pages. As near as he could tell, they were filled. It didn't matter. He'd find a way to make time for her.

Pushing the calendar away, he turned to face her. "Whenever's convenient for you."

The word *convenient* didn't fit the situation. There was nothing convenient about it. "Mrs. Dalton got the court to accelerate the date, so as soon as possible would be very much appreciated." She eyed him hopefully. "I can come back with the papers later this afternoon if you like."

He would have liked to say yes, but he couldn't. "I'm leaving for court in half an hour." And more than likely would be there for the rest of the day, until the judge adjourned the proceedings.

Lilli didn't allow obstacles to deter her, not anymore. She'd learned that along the way as she carved out a living for herself and her son. The meek and mild were stepped on, the forceful were not.

"All right, then I can drop the documents off at your place tonight," she suggested. "I know it sounds like I'm being pushy, but I'll feel a lot better the sooner you have all the ammunition you need at your disposal." And then she realized that she'd overlooked an important, salient point. "Unless your wife doesn't like work from the office showing up on your doorstep at night."

"No wife."

The disclaimer was out of his mouth before he realized that he had just ruined his one opportunity to keep her permanently at arm's length. If Lilli thought he was married, she would keep her distance. She wasn't some femme fatale, given to whimsical flirting. There wouldn't be any more impromptu incidents of her throwing her arms around his neck. Lilli was honorable that way.

How the hell did he really know *what* she was like, he silently demanded the next moment, growing irritable. He hadn't been right about her the first time around. Eight years ago he would have bet his last dime—and his life—that Lilli wasn't the type to vanish without a word, especially after someone had bared his soul to her.

He would have lost that bet.

For all he knew, the challenge of prying a man away from his wife would spur Lilli on.

I really didn't know you at all, did I? he thought, looking at her.

"You're not married?" Lilli asked, surprised. Someone like Kullen should have gotten snapped up years ago. He was one of the few true good guys left in the world. They didn't make men like him anymore. If she hadn't discovered that she was pregnant the same evening that he'd proposed, she would have gladly married him and spent the rest of her life trying to put that one awful episode in her life behind her.

Don't go there, she warned herself. *What's done is done.*

"No," he answered, "I'm not married."

"Oh."

Despite the fact that it was years too late for her, that what *could* have been between them was in the past, Lilli was suddenly aware of a small, intense flame of warmth igniting within her. A warmth that swiftly spread, as if to thaw her out. To make her feel alive again.

This wouldn't accomplish anything, she upbraided herself. It was best to leave things just the way they were. There was no going back. Her future, her life, was all bound up around the boy. Jonathan was the important one here. Jonathan was the *only* reason she was here, temporarily interacting with Kullen.

She wanted to be clear that he didn't mind her doing this. Eager though she was, she didn't want to risk crowding him. "Then I can bring the papers by your house?"

He didn't want her getting the wrong idea, that her coming over would lead to anything but discussing her case.

"You could have brought them by even if I was married," he informed her. "When's the court date?" She told him and he whistled, shaking his head. No wonder she was antsy. "Two weeks. That really doesn't leave much time," he agreed.

"That's the whole idea behind such an early court date. Mrs. Dalton's trying to steamroll right over me."

Kullen liked a challenge, liked fighting the good fight. Cut-and-dried cases didn't allow him to stretch his muscles, and a lot of the time they bored him. His gut told him he wouldn't be bored with this case. Not by a long shot.

"Well, Mrs. Dalton's just going to have to rethink her strategy," he replied. He reached over a pile of papers to get one of his business cards from his desk. Flipping it over, he wrote down his home address on the back, then held the card out to Lilli. "Here's my address," he told her. "I should be home after six."

What sort of a home did he live in? Was it strictly utilitarian, the way his room had been in college? Or had his obvious success changed him, changed his tastes? Was his home big and splashy, filled with furniture and objects of art chosen by some interior decorator?

Lilli slipped the card into her purse. "I'll be there," she promised.

She started to open the door, but the sound of his voice stopped her.

"Just out of curiosity, who referred you to me?"

He wondered if she'd just looked him up, forgetting that he'd once had plans to work in the poorer section of Los Angeles, counseling those who couldn't afford to pay a lawyer. Or if she did remember, did finding him here make her think that he'd sold out and joined his father's firm just to please him?

Her answer caught him off guard. "Your mother."

"My mother?" Damn it, Kate had been right. Now that she, Nikki and Jewel were all squared away with fiancés and weddings in the near future, Theresa Manetti had decided to turn her sights on him. "You looked up my mother?" he asked incredulously.

"No, actually, it's all just a very fortunate coincidence."

Yeah, I just bet, Kullen thought. He didn't believe in coincidences, fate or luck. Not anymore. Especially not where his mother was concerned. She'd known about this at lunch today and she hadn't said a word to him.

"My mother needed to have a party catered," Lilli explained, "and *she* looked up your mother. Your mother comes very highly recommended," she told him by way of a compliment. His expression remained oddly stoic. "They started talking and my mother told yours that I was badly in need of a lawyer. Your mother volunteered you."

His mother probably heard the words "my single daughter" and her imagination galloped off, Kullen thought darkly. "Did my mother ask yours what kind of lawyer you needed?"

Lilli smiled. It was the same smile he used to think lit up a dark room. "My mother only said I needed a good one. Your mother proudly said that you were. But my nine months in law school were not wasted," she said, tongue in cheek. "I looked you up," she told him. "I wanted to be sure that you weren't practicing criminal law or just doing estate planning." A distant expression came into her eyes. "I won't need a criminal lawyer except maybe as a last resort."

He knew what she was saying. That if it came down to it, she'd kill to keep her son. He wondered if she actually meant that.

"As your lawyer, I have to advise you not to make those kind of *jokes* right now—" he underscored the word "—just in case Elizabeth Dalton does happen to turn up dead."

Lilli studied him for a long moment. "I don't remember you being this cautious before."

He was the exact opposite of cautious and serious when it came to his social life, but professionally it was another matter. The law didn't leave a lot of wiggle room for mistakes.

"I'm not," he replied. "But in this particular case, it wouldn't hurt to cover all bases."

He was right and she was grateful to him for that. For taking her case. The last thing she wanted was for him to think she was criticizing him or his methods.

"Thank you," she said again. "Just knowing that you're on the case makes me feel a great deal better already."

"That makes one of us," he said to the door after she had left and closed it.

Damn it, he had a feeling that once this case was over he would have to start from scratch again. He would have to work to drive her essence out of his head. Out of his soul.

"Of all the law firms in Bedford, she had to wander into mine," he murmured under his breath, riffing on Humphrey Bogart's famous line in *Casablanca*.

With a sigh Kullen glanced down at his watch. He gave Lilli five minutes to stop at Selma's desk, get the list he'd suggested she take with her and then make her way to the elevator.

Exactly five minutes later, he opened his door and strode over to Kate's office two doors down. Reaching it he knocked exactly once on the frosted glass. Too impatient to wait the mega-second for a response, he opened the door and walked in.

Books were spread out and open all over his sister's desk.

Engrossed in her research, Kate looked up sharply when she heard him walk in. "I didn't say come in."

"But you would have," he pointed out glibly.

"I could have been with a client—or making out with Jackson," she answered.

He shrugged, closing the door behind him. "Then you would have thrown me out and I would have waited in the hall."

"Waited," she repeated mockingly. "You don't know how to wait. This sounds serious." She pushed the book in front of her aside. "What's up?"

"Did you know about this?" he demanded.

"Well," she said carefully, "that all depends."

"On what?" he asked her suspiciously, his eyes narrowing as he scrutinized her.

"On what 'this' means. If you're asking about Selma's birthday, yes, I know about it. Actually, I was the one who found out that it's next week—"

Raising his voice, he cut in. "I'm not talking about Selma's birthday." He was exasperated. When she got all wound up, Kate could fire more words per second than any living human. He knew from experience that he only had a couple of seconds to get out in front of that before she picked up her pace. "I'm talking about my newest client."

"You have a new client," Kate deadpanned. "How nice for you." She shook her head. "Right now, my plate is so full that if you're trying to palm him—"

"It's a her," he corrected.

"Her," she amended without losing a beat, "off on me, I just might be tempted to kill you, and then Jackson is going to have to marry me quickly so I can get conjugal rights in prison."

He was trying to pin her down and she was making jokes, he thought darkly. "So then you don't know about her."

"I might," Kate allowed. "Depending on what her name is. Is it somebody famous?" She looked at Kullen more closely. "Kullen, you're scaring me. Why aren't you talking?" Leaning forward, she gave him her full attention. "Just who is your new client, Kullen?"

For a second, because he didn't want to go into explanations, he debated just turning around and walking out. But if he did that, his sister's curiosity would go into overdrive and she would hound him until he *did* tell her.

So he watched Kate's face as he said, "It's Lilli Mc-Call."

The name didn't seem to mean anything to her.

"Okay," Kate said, drawing out the single word as if it was comprised of four syllables. She waited for something more substantial to follow.

"You're not familiar with her name?" he pressed suspiciously.

"Should I be?"

Granted, he'd never talked about Lilli, preferring eight years ago to keep her to himself like some special treasure that he'd mined by accident. And then, when she had done her vanishing act, he'd never told anyone about her because then he would have had to admit that she'd devastated him.

So his secret love remained a secret.

Or so he'd thought at the time.

But even so, he figured that Kate with her insidious way of delving into everything, especially *his* business, would have sensed that something was up, which would have led her to find out about Lilli.

Maybe he'd given his sister too much credit.

Or maybe, just maybe, for once in her life she'd respected his privacy the way he really didn't respect hers. Everything was fair when it came to siblings, at least that had always been his rule of thumb. He'd invoked it because he did care about Kate, and acting as if he had the right to know everything that concerned her just made it easier to watch over her.

But now the tables had turned and it was *his* life that was caught in his mother's crosshairs.

And he didn't like it one damn bit.

Rather than label Lilli as a woman from his past, or more accurately, *the* woman from his past, he said only one salient thing.

"Mom referred her."

Kate's grin materialized on her lips at the speed of light. "Well, like you once said, everyone needs a hobby."

He scowled. "That was when she was bugging you, not me."

Kate seemed to take pity on him. She was too happy these days to be vindictive. "Well, I've got to admit that Mom's taste is pretty good. Why don't you give this woman a chance once you've handled her, um, case," she concluded with a wicked wink.

"I already did once."

"You fooled around with a client at your initial meeting?" Kate asked him, stunned.

"No," he bit off in disgust.

"Enlighten me. Exactly what do you mean, you already did once?"

He waved his hand dismissively. "Never mind," he retorted. "Just tell Mom to stick to catering and not matchmaking."

"Sorry," Kate called after him as he walked out. "She won't listen to me if I say that. Under the circumstances, I don't have a leg to stand on."

That made two of them, because his own legs felt wobblier than hell right now. Eight years and she still had that kind of effect on him, despite everything that had happened.

He closed his eyes and sighed. He should have gone on vacation this week the way he had initially planned. Served him right. If he'd taken that holiday, then his mother, with her soft, chewy-on-the-inside, chewy-on-the-outside heart would have volunteered Kate to help Lilli with her case, and he could have gone on his way, mercifully in the dark, his world on an even keel.

Instead, he felt as if he were sitting on top of the San Andreas Fault, shaken up for all he was worth. And for what? Once this was over, once he won exclusive custody of her son for her, Lilli would be on her way again.

On her way and out of his life.

She'd done it once—there was no reason to believe she wouldn't do it again.

He told himself to remember that if he felt his "hands-off" resolve weakening anytime in the foreseeable future.

Chapter Five

Lilli saw that her mother's car was parked in the driveway when she pulled up to her house.

Given the hour, that meant that her mother had already picked Jonathan up from school and returned. It was amazing how easily all three of them had adjusted to this routine. Less than a month ago, she and Jonathan had been living near Santa Barbara, cocooned by the almost idyllic life there. Erik Dalton had been dead for four months and she was adjusting to the idea that she didn't have to worry about him suddenly turning up on her doorstep and for some twisted reason beyond comprehension, demanding access to his son.

Then Elizabeth Dalton had happened and everything she'd always feared came to fruition. Lilli had packed up, sold everything and come back to her hometown. She knew she couldn't hide, but she felt that she needed her mother's moral support in order to fend off the other woman.

She'd worried about Jonathan adjusting to being uprooted this way, but she realized now that she needn't have. Unlike his father, Jonathan was happy, easygoing and even-tempered, and she was immensely grateful for that.

The moment she put the key in the door, Jonathan came running.

"Hi, sweetheart." She greeted the light of her life with a fierce hug. It was returned.

Someday, all too soon, that would change. Preteen boys didn't think it was cool to pal around with their mothers. But for now, she would enjoy his affection for all it was worth.

"Know where your grandmother is?" she asked him. He pointed toward the kitchen. "Thanks. As you were," she told him. This week, Jonathan was considering soldiering as a career choice, so she played along. Last week, he'd thought he might give ranching a try and she had gotten a book on the different breeds of horses for him. She was going to be a hands-on mother all the way, she thought, heading for the kitchen.

Maybe, if Erik's mother had been that way, he wouldn't have turned out to be so despicable. But then, she reminded herself, she wouldn't have Jonathan in her life.

Everything happens for a reason. Everything but losing Jonathan, she amended fiercely. *That* was never going to happen.

Her mother came out of the kitchen. "I thought I heard you."

"Hi, Mom. Do you think you can stay a little longer? I'm not in for the night yet," she told the older, petite woman as she headed for the room that she'd claimed as her office. It was still very much in a state of disarray, with boxes piled up in the corner.

She tried to remember which carton she'd packed the metal box in. It contained all their important documents. She'd done that so that if there was ever a natural disaster, all she had to do was grab one box—after she grabbed Jonathan.

Following her only child into the small room off the kitchen, Anne McCall asked, "Did you see him?"

Lilli knew that the "him" her mother referred to was Kullen.

"Yes," she answered, opening up the carton closest to her. "I saw him." The metal box wasn't in it. She shoved the carton aside.

"And?"

Lilli turned her attention to the next carton. She struck out again. "And he's going to take the case."

Anne shifted around so that she could see her daughter's face. "And?"

Third time was the charm. With a triumphant sigh, Lilli removed the dark gray metal box from the last carton she'd opened. In the background, she heard the familiar, soothing theme song of one of Jonathan's favorite afternoon programs, an imaginative show where a robot given to self-repairing took his viewers through the vivid pages of history.

As she opened the metal box, Lilli glanced at her mother.

"And?" she echoed, unclear as to what her mother

was driving at. She took a guess. "And he told me he thinks we have a good chance to win even though the woman is—" she dropped her voice and came closer to her mother, not wanting to take a chance that Jonathan might overhear her "—the first known recorded case of a barracuda without fins."

Despite the fact that the woman was making her life a living hell, Lilli was not about to bad-mouth Elizabeth—or the man who had, through no desire of his own, been his father. Jonathan deserved better than that. She wanted her son to grow up exposed to as little hatred as was humanly possible. God knew there would be time enough for him to see what the world could be like when he became an adult.

Her mother continued to eye her. Lilli got the distinct impression that she was waiting for something more.

And then she asked, "Didn't you say that you once dated him?"

Caught completely off guard when her mother had produced Kullen's name out of the blue, saying that she had a referral from a reliable source that Kullen Manetti was an excellent lawyer, Lilli had been forced to explain why she'd appeared so stunned. She had fallen back on a half truth. She'd admitted that she'd known him in college and that they'd gone out a couple of times. She had deliberately avoided telling her mother that Kullen had proposed to her and that she'd left town right after that.

She had left not because she'd discovered that she was pregnant, but because she had been afraid that she would allow her fears to get the better of her and would say yes to Kullen. And then she would have had to tell him that the baby wasn't his. To have allowed him to think that he was the father would have been the very height of deception. She'd had no doubt that Kullen would have always wondered if she'd married him because she'd loved him, or as a matter of convenience. That would be no way to run a marriage.

So she'd left. Left without telling him anything because it was too hard to share the shame of what had happened. Or worse, for him to have insisted on going through with the wedding and marrying her out of pity.

She knew logically that none of this had been her fault, but somehow, she still felt as if it was.

Until she held Jonathan in her arms.

The moment she looked down into his small, perfect little face, the love that welled up within her drove out everything—guilt, shame, anger. All that remained was love.

And that love was fiercely protective. No way in hell was she going to allow Elizabeth Dalton to get her grasping, perfectly manicured hands on Jonathan.

"Yes," she admitted, "I did say that." She was in no mood for a chorus of "Matchmaker, Matchmaker, Make Me A Match." "Mother," she said pointedly, "I'm up to my neck in the fight of my life. This is no time to play the dating game."

Never one to push, Anne nodded. "I'm sorry, dear, you're right. I was just looking for a way to divert you and alleviate your tension."

Having retrieved Jonathan's birth certificate, Lilli took out several other legal documents and began to feed them into the scanner. She wasn't about to take a chance on losing anything.

"What would really alleviate my tension," she told her mother, "is if that woman would disappear from the face of the earth."

"You know," Anne began thoughtfully, "my cousin Sal knows a few people who—"

Dear God, her mother wasn't taking her seriously, was she? "Mother!" Lilli cried sharply.

"Just kidding," Anne countered. "Sadly, the only people my cousin Sal knows are gambling addicts. They wouldn't be any help in a situation like this." She watched as Lilli scanned another document. In less than a minute, the printer spit out a perfect copy. "What is it you're doing?" she asked.

"I told Kullen that I'd bring by these documents he wanted tonight."

A note of concern entered Anne's voice. "You're going to his office at night?" While Bedford had been deemed one of the safest cities in the country with a population of over one hundred thousand for several years in a row now, Anne was never one to tempt fate.

Lilli briefly thought of just nodding and letting the matter go, allowing her mother to think that she was going back to meet with Kullen in his office. But that would be lying, if only by omission, and she didn't believe in lying. The most she ever did was keep her own counsel, refraining from going into detail. Even her mother didn't know the full story surrounding Jonathan's conception. Mercifully, her mother respected her privacy. She couldn't pay her back by letting her believe what wasn't true.

"I'm bringing these over to his house." Another sheet emerged from the printer and she added it to the others.

"Oh."

Lilli's head shot up. The two-letter word sounded far more pregnant than she had ever been. "Not *oh,* Mom. It's just more convenient that way, that's all."

Anne nodded, a knowing smile curving her mouth. "Yes, I know."

No, you don't. "Kullen needs to get up to speed as fast as possible."

Anne seemed to struggle to keep the grin from taking over her entire face. "And can he? Get up to speed fast?"

All that was missing was a nudge-nudge, wink-wink comment. "Mother, if you're asking me if I ever slept with Kullen Manetti, no, I never slept with him."

Anne held up her hands as if to innocently fend off another volley of words. "I didn't ask."

"Not in so many words," Lilli allowed, "but, yes, you did."

Anne sighed, shaking her head. It was obvious her mother's heart literally *ached* to see her look so upset.

She sighed. "Too bad that you and Erik weren't able to work things out. Then, even though he died in that accident, maybe all this could have been avoided."

She'd never told her mother the circumstances involved in her getting pregnant. The words rose up now, scratching her throat, trying to get free. But if her mother knew the truth, it would only cause her anguish. And although Lilli would feel better finally telling someone, finally getting it all out in the open, she couldn't do it at the price of wounding her mother.

So she kept her peace and nodded. "Yes, too bad. But all that's water under the bridge, as Grandma used to say. And who knows, Mrs. Dalton might have still wanted to fight me for Jonathan's custody. She lost her only son and she seems to think that you can replace one person with another as long as the gene pool is basically the same."

Slightly shorter than her daughter, Anne ran her hand over her daughter's blond hair, an endless font of love evident in the simple gesture.

"Sure you don't want me to go over there and have a talk with her?" she offered. "I'm more than willing to do it."

Lilli laughed, shaking her head. "No thanks, Mom. One battle in court is about all I can handle at a time. There's no telling what you might do. I saw you get angry once," she recalled. "Not a pretty sight."

"Offer's on the table anytime you want to take me up on it, honey."

Finished copying, Lilli filed the copies of the documents in a light blue folder. Leaving the folder on her desk, she rounded it and put her arms around her mother.

"Thanks, Mom, I'll keep that in mind." Lilli gave the older woman a quick, heartfelt hug. "You're the best, Mom."

"Glad you finally noticed that," Anne said with just the right amount of dryness. "And don't worry about hurrying back," she said as Lilli turned toward the desk again and slipped the documents she'd just compiled into the recesses of her large black rectangular purse. The latter could have doubled as a briefcase and not a small one, either. "I was thinking about spending the night here anyway." Her mother's light blue eyes seemed to dance as she told her, "I brought some of your old storybooks over to read to Jonathan."

Lilli smiled warmly and predicted, "He'll get a big kick out of that."

"So will I," Anne confessed. "When I'm not tearing up," she added. She watched her daughter zip up the purse. "Got everything?" she pressed.

"Everything," Lilli echoed, taking no offense at her mother double-checking her. She was only acting out of concern. Lilli hefted the purse and slid it onto her right shoulder.

"Then, good luck," Anne said, following her to the front door.

Passing the family room, Lilli stopped for a moment, peering in. She wondered if it was normal to have her heart swell every time she looked at her son. "I've got to go out again, Jonathan. But I'll be back soon." She knew he liked her to touch base with him. "Don't forget your homework."

Jonathan pretended to hang his head, like a prisoner sentenced to twenty years hard labor. "I won't forget, Mom."

Lilli turned toward her mother. "And don't you do it for him, either," she warned.

Anne's nearly unlined face was the picture of innocence. "Wouldn't dream of it."

A small laugh escaped Lilli's lips. "I don't believe you." Her mother was a pushover and they both knew it. Moreover, Jonathan knew it. But it was time to go. "I love you," she called out to her son.

"Love you back," Jonathan answered, his attention already back to the robot on the screen.

Who could ask for more than this? Lilli smiled as she went out the front door. Whatever it took, she would keep that boy in her life.

Rather than terminate early, court had taken longer than Kullen had counted on.

And then, leaving, he'd gotten tangled up in the traffic jam from hell. His temper, usually level, was definitely the worse for wear tonight.

He needed to unwind.

He didn't have the luxury.

Kullen had been in his house exactly three minutes when the doorbell rang. The kid from the pizzeria had to have made every single light, he thought.

He'd ordered takeout on his way home. The restaurant's number was one of the first on speed dial on both his cell phone and his landline at home. Convenience was a high priority for him, given his drive-by lifestyle.

Digging money out of his wallet, Kullen crossed back to the foyer. He threw open the front door, holding up two twenties.

"I thought I was supposed to pay you," Lilli said drily. And then she made the only logical assumption from the look of surprise on his face. "You forgot I was coming by with the papers, didn't you?"

He hadn't forgotten. How could he? Lilli had been on his mind all afternoon, creeping, entirely unbidden, into his thoughts. During the court case, images of Lilli, past and present, kept materializing in his mind's eye. Being on his game had been particularly difficult this afternoon.

"I ordered takeout," he told her. "I thought the delivery boy would be here before you."

"More restaurant food?" she asked as she entered. She made it personal before she could think not to. "Don't you ever have anything healthy to eat?"

"Pizza's healthy," he countered, arguing like a true lawyer. "It has all the major food groups," he said when she looked at him skeptically. "Cheese, tomatoes, meat, bread," he enumerated.

"And a ton of salt." And that negated anything good the pizza might have to bring to the table.

"That's what makes it edible."

For a moment, she was propelled back into the past. The past when she had finally succeeded in banking down her demons and had thought that maybe, just maybe, she would be able to find a little happiness with Kullen.

Before the roof caved in on her world and she discovered she was pregnant.

The next beat, the moment was gone.

"What do you have in your refrigerator?" she asked. Maybe she could come up with some kind of dinner for him. Almost anything was better than pizza, temptingly aromatic though it was.

"Shelves."

It was hard not to laugh. "Anything on those shelves?"

He thought for a second, envisioning the inside of the refrigerator the last time he'd looked. "A couple of leftover takeout things that I'm debating donating to science."

She grinned, oblivious to the fondness that had slipped into her voice. "You never learned how to cook, did you?"

There was nothing wrong with that. He knew lots of people who didn't cook. That was why God had made restaurants.

"Never saw the purpose," he told her. "Besides, most days I either order in or go out for lunch. Same applies to dinner."

She shook her head. "It's not healthy to live like that." The doorbell rang and he went to answer it. "The people in Tibet don't eat takeout and they live a very long life," she said, refusing to let up, "subsisting on yogurt and vegetables."

He laughed shortly. "It's not a long life, it only *seems* like a long life because they can't find a decent steak."

This time, it was the delivery boy with his pizza. Kullen handed him the money, then took possession of the extra-large pizza. He turned around and closed the door with his back.

"I ordered pizza with everything," he told her, carrying it back to the dining room on the other side of the family room. "You see something you don't like, just take it off."

She tried not to think what a loaded phrase that actually was. "What if I don't like anything on it?" Lilli posed.

Kullen never missed a beat. "More for me." He set

the box down on the dining room table. "But I seem to remember that pizza was your weakness."

No, you were my weakness, she thought. *But that Lilli had to disappear a long time ago.*

Kullen opened the box and the aroma, already leaching out of the box by any means possible, now robustly filled the air, arousing her dormant taste buds.

"It does smell good," she conceded.

"Help yourself," he said, gesturing toward the oil-soaked box. "I'll get the plates and napkins."

"I'll get them," she offered. It was the least she could do. "Just tell me where the kitchen is."

"You can't miss it. It's the only room with a refrigerator in it," he deadpanned. And then, when she kept on looking at him, he pointed over to the area just beyond the living room.

"Wise guy."

A sense of déjà vu washed over him as he watched Lilli disappear around the corner. It brought with it a host of warm, soft memories that in turn aroused feelings that had long since slipped into exile.

Don't go there, don't go there, he warned himself.

But he knew that was easier said than done. He'd already crossed the line once. And each time it would get easier.

And all the more difficult to come back.

Chapter Six

They were doing justice to the pizza. Kullen had a hunch that they would. It was almost like old times.

Almost.

It would be easy, so seductively easy, to let his guard drop. To allow that feeling to overtake him, the one that had whispered that this was like old times—the times when he had struggled so hard to create and win. And finally had.

He had fallen for her the very first moment he'd ever laid eyes on her. The first time he'd glimpsed her face with its regal, aristocratic lines and felt his stomach muscles tighten into a knot so hard, he could scarcely breathe. There was no question in his mind that Lilli McCall was easily the most beautiful creature he'd ever seen.

But back then, his "pre-shallow period" as Kate referred to it, it had taken more than just looks, no matter

how incredible, to captivate him. What had drawn him
in was the sadness in her eyes. It made him ache for her
and want to erase her pain. He had launched a full-scale,
albeit subtle campaign to get to know her, to get close
to her, a feat his best friend at the time, Gil Davis, had
warned him was doomed to failure. Gil had had his finger on the pulse of the campus social circles and he'd
said that Lilli McCall was a loner, a serious, self-contained fortress. Word was that *no* one really got close
to her.

It was a challenge Kullen couldn't refuse.

And the more he'd worked at getting closer, the more
he'd found his own defenses going down. In the space
of a few days Lilli had stopped being a challenge and
had begun being someone he just wanted to help. Someone he was determined to get to trust him. They'd had
several classes together and had been in the same study
group. The latter had turned out to be his first triumph
with her.

"C'mon," he'd urged her cheerfully and relentlessly.
"Law school's tough. This is a communal effort to help
us all survive. What one of us doesn't know, maybe
someone else does. It's a give-and-take situation." It had
been his eyes that had held her, he'd later discovered,
not any physical touch of the hand, something that she'd
avoided religiously then. "You can't deny us the benefit
of your brain, can you?" he remembered coaxing.

When she'd finally, somewhat reluctantly agreed to
study with him, he had wanted to shout his victory from
the rooftops, but prudently refrained, pretending to take
it all in stride.

That had been the real beginning. The beginning of

what in time had turned out to be an all-too-short relationship that had, on the outside, held such promise.

He could still remember the first time he'd made her smile, the first time he'd heard the sound of her laughter.

And the first time she hadn't stiffened when he'd kissed her.

There was no way to measure the intensity of the feelings he'd had for her. Feelings he would have bet his life were returned. In the short time they were together, he'd bared his soul to her and caught just the tiniest glimpses of hers. It had by no means been a balanced exchange, but that was okay. With Lilli things were different, all the rules were thrown out and new ones had taken their place. He was fine with taking the tiny, baby steps. As long as they eventually led to his goal.

He'd been so sure, so very sure that they would.

Which was why his entire world had fallen apart when she had disappeared from his life.

At first, he'd thought that Lilli had been kidnapped. He was incredibly, stupidly certain that the woman he loved above everything else on earth wouldn't have just taken off on him. Especially not after he'd proposed to her.

But she had.

Lilli had just disappeared, leaving a note on his desk. The note had fallen on the floor between the wastepaper basket and his desk. He hadn't found it until, lost in a frenzy of frustration and helpless anger, he'd kicked the wastepaper basket aside. Falling over, it had spilled its contents, but it was then that he'd seen the small white note card with two words in her handwriting. Two words that twisted a knife right into his chest.

"I'm sorry." That was all she'd written. Just, "I'm sorry." And that was supposed to explain her departure and compel him to go on living his life. A life that no longer contained her.

Sitting opposite Lilli now in his dining room, a room he rarely used except when he needed to spread out a massive collection of legal papers, it all came back to him with the force of a detonating bomb. Everything he'd felt, everything he'd gone through with her and then, without her. The good, the bad and, finally, the anger. He'd been a fool because he'd loved her and would have done anything for her. She hadn't cared enough to explain things face-to-face.

But now, after all these years, he had his answer. He knew why she'd left.

Even so, he wanted to ask her why she'd tossed him aside like some kind of used tissue, without the courtesy of an explanation.

Without a chance to fight for her and prove he was the better man.

The words vibrated on his lips. But after all this time, he had his answer. It was cruelly obvious. Lilli had abandoned him for Erik Dalton, the only heir to an incredible fortune that he had done nothing to deserve. The rumor was that he had never been turned down, especially not by a woman. A morally bankrupt playboy who was the very poster child for the stereotypical rich kid with a heart of lead, Erik Dalton had gotten every woman he had ever set his sights on.

All he had to do was crook his finger and women

fell from the sky, eager for his attention, eager to have some of his generosity touch their lives. He went through money as if it was of no consequence to him. There was always more.

Was that it? Kullen wondered now. Had Lilli been blinded and won over by the allure of materialistic goods? He'd always seen her as pure and unfazed by material wealth. It was obvious now that he'd been blinded, too. Blinded by his feelings.

Had there been a price tag on her affections after all?

The Lilli McCall he'd loved so fiercely had been an honorable woman. But then, the Lilli he'd loved would have never abruptly left him with a marriage proposal still warm on his lips.

"Why are you fighting this?" he asked her quietly, without preamble.

Polishing off her third slice of pizza and finally feeling full, Lilli looked up at him sharply. The question had come out of the blue and she didn't know what he was referring to. The first thing that occurred to her by "this" was that the feelings were still there, carefully encased in Bubble Wrap and stored away. Feelings that belonged exclusively to him.

So Lilli waited for him to elaborate and prayed that she could answer him without raking over old scars.

"I could try to broker an arrangement between you and Elizabeth Dalton for joint custody. Lay down a few ground rules—"

Lilli continued staring at him, growing more stunned. Why was he saying this? Had that dreadful woman's lawyers gotten to him, bought him off? She hadn't thought that would be possible, but now she wasn't so sure.

Wasn't there anyplace left for her to turn to?

"No," Lilli said firmly before he could continue, then repeated the word in a louder voice. "No!"

"Heard you the first time," Kullen assured her matter-of-factly. And he grew serious, leaning over the table. Leaning closer to her. His eyes pinned her down. "Now, tell me why."

Her eyes darted along his face, as if trying to fathom the secret behind Kullen's words. Finally, she asked, "Why what?"

"Why you're so against this when obviously, at one point, you must have been all for it. To hitch your star to the Dalton fortune." She opened her mouth to speak but he talked louder and faster. The cynicism was impossible to miss. "I mean, the lure of all that money, the comfort it could bring—hard to imagine turning your back on all that. It had to be a whole different world for you. For anyone. The kind of money the Daltons have is the stuff that fairy tales are made of."

Oh, God.

She pressed her hand against her abdomen, certain she was going to be sick. "They got to you, didn't they?"

Kullen's dark blue eyes were cold. Flat. And accusing. "Not to me."

There was an allegation in his voice, and it didn't take much for her to get his drift. She began to protest. "But I don't—"

He cut her short, not wanting her to lie. "Oh, come on, Lilli. I'm your lawyer. If I'm going to be of any use to you, you have to level with me," he insisted sharply. Angrily. "Tell me everything." His mouth curved cynically. "Why aren't you still part of the Dalton's happy little family?"

How could he say that to her? Did he think she was some kind of gold digger? The one person, aside from her mother, who she thought knew her, accused her of being this awful person. It hurt more than she thought possible.

Lilli pushed her chair away from the table and stood up. She had to get out of here. "I'm sorry, coming to you was a mistake." She picked up her manila envelope. He wouldn't be needing them anymore. "This has been a waste of time for both of us—"

Kullen told himself that he should just let her walk out. It was in his best interest. Another man would have sat back and watched this little drama unfold, feeling a sense of vindication. Payback, as the old saying went, was a bitch. And she had earned her payback.

But he wasn't another man. For better or for worse, he was who and what he was: The man who had once loved Lilli McCall with his entire heart and soul. Even now, he couldn't avenge himself by leaving her to twist in the wind. She had come to him looking for help.

Kullen was on his feet, rounding the table and blocking her exit from the room. "I need the truth from you, Lilli. I need to know why someone like you would have gotten mixed up with someone like Erik Dalton in the first place. He had a reputation as the biggest womanizer around. I thought you were different—"

"I was," she insisted. Which was why she was so

haunted by what had happened. Why it had been so hard for her to get past it in the first place.

His eyes narrowed as he looked right into her. Aware that he was still holding her in place, Kullen dropped his hands from her shoulders. "Convince me."

For a long moment, she said nothing and he thought she would walk out after all. But then she sighed as she pressed her lips together. He wanted to shake her, to shout at her and demand to know why she'd slept with a man like Erik Dalton when he'd had to work so hard to get her to trust him. To get her *not* to freeze up when he touched her.

That look in her eyes was back. That look that echoed an unfathomable sadness.

Kullen wanted to hold her more than anything in the world.

But he didn't.

His hands remained at his sides. He waited for the explanation he felt he had coming to him.

There was a slight tremor in her voice as she said, "I suppose I have this coming."

"We'll talk about that later. Answer my question, Lilli."

Every word ached. "I didn't leave because I wanted to, Kullen."

"Leave who?" he demanded. Was she talking about the father of her baby? Had he pushed her away when she told him she was pregnant? And why did that thought hold not the slightest bit of satisfaction for him? She'd left him and Erik had left her. That was supposed to be poetic justice. So why wasn't it? "Leave Erik?"

She stared at him. "No, leave you."

"Then why did you?"

"Because I had to." Her voice throbbed with anguish. "I didn't want to see your anger or your pity." She pressed her lips together again, trying not to cry. "I couldn't deal with that."

"You're going to have to be a little clearer than that, Lilli." She looked as if she wanted to flee, he thought. He knew he couldn't hold her against her will, but nonetheless, the idea was tempting. More than anything, he wanted her to make him understand why things had turned out the way they had.

Every word cost her. She didn't want to look back into the past, into the abyss of mistakes that had been made. "I didn't leave you because I was going to Erik. I left you *because* of Erik."

"Clearer," he instructed again, stone-faced.

The breath Lilli let out was shaky. "I was pregnant."

Kullen's expression hardened. Every time he thought of Lilli with that worthless bastard…when their own relationship hadn't gone beyond heated kisses, at her request, a request he'd respected….

"We've already established that," he said.

She didn't know how to tell him. She'd blocked all thoughts, all memory of events for so long. "The day you asked me to marry you was the best and the worst day of my life."

The word *worst* jumped up at him, lit in glaring neon lights. "Nice to know I've still got it," he said sarcastically.

She pushed on, knowing that she had to make him understand. She was afraid that he would stand by his word and not help her if she didn't tell him everything. But, oh, it was so hard.

"It was the best day because I found someone good, someone who could make me forget. Someone I loved." He looked at her sharply. She pushed on. "And the worst day because I found out I was pregnant."

As her words pierced his heart, he came to the only conclusion he could. "You mean you were seeing Erik Dalton while we—"

"No," she retorted. "Erik *happened* before I met you and there was no 'seeing' involved, no dating, if that's what you mean."

Lilli stopped, momentarily too emotional to continue because she was reliving the horrible incident that had all but destroyed her life and turned her entire world upside down.

She looked as if she was going to bolt.

Not until you finish telling me. Kullen gently put his hands on her shoulders. He could literally *feel* her anguish, could sense her being torn between telling him and keeping silent.

"Tell me," he urged quietly.

The war within her was reflected in her eyes. And then, she squared her shoulders, as if she were about to go into battle.

When she finally spoke, her voice was firm, quiet. Almost oddly removed.

"My first year in law school, I forced myself to accept an invitation to a frat party. I was so terribly shy and I knew I had to make an effort to get out of my shell." A sad smile played along her lips. "I mean, who wants a painfully shy lawyer, right? There were a lot of people at the party…." Her voice trailed off.

"Including Erik?" he prodded.

She nodded. "Erik was there. He seemed nice, attentive." Every word took effort to say. "Almost sweet." A rueful sound accompanied the description. "Somewhere in the middle of the evening, he suggested that we go somewhere more private, get a 'real' drink." She stopped.

"And you went with him?" He'd always pictured her being innocent, but never naive.

Lilli raised her chin defiantly. "No, I didn't. I told him I had to get back home because I had a paper I needed to finish for Monday. He told me he could get a paper on any topic under the sun, and that shouldn't interrupt the good time we were having."

She shrugged helplessly, wishing she could change the rest of the narrative. Wishing that it had never happened. But that would mean she'd have to wish away Jonathan and she could never do that.

"I told him I wouldn't feel right about that. That I needed to earn my grade. He laughed and said I was a rare person. I left the party and went home. None of the other girls I lived with were there." She paused for a moment, taking a shaky breath. "He followed me. When the doorbell rang, I thought one of my roommates had forgotten her key. But it was Erik. He pushed his way in…." Her voice broke.

The horror of the situation suddenly hit Kullen with the force of an anvil dropping on his head. He called himself seven kinds of a jackass. Here he'd been feeling sorry for himself for loving her, and all along she'd been a victim.

"He raped you?" Kullen asked, struggling to contain his outrage.

She drew her lips together in a thin line, then nodded.

He stared at her, stunned. "Why didn't you report him to the police?"

"Because I was ashamed." It was so hard not to cry. Talking had sharpened all the edges of the incident. She could feel them all pricking her flesh again. "It would have been just my word against his. People saw him at the party talking to me. Walking me out to my car. They'd think that the sex was consensual and that I cried rape after the fact because he wouldn't allow himself to be blackmailed."

It seemed too fantastic for words, but Kullen was acutely aware of the dead man's reputation. "Is that what he said?"

She nodded, avoiding his eyes. "He told me it was my fault. That I'd asked for it and that I couldn't expect a guy to shut down after I 'got his engine going.'" She drew in another shaky breath. "All I wanted to do was forget that it ever happened." She smiled at Kullen and it all but broke his heart. "You almost made me forget. And then I found out I was pregnant—"

"Why didn't you tell me?" He would have taken care of her—after he'd beaten that scum to a pulp.

"Because I didn't want you to look at me with disgust, or pity—"

"So letting me think that something was wrong, that you'd rather run away and disappear than marry me, was better?" he demanded. She made no answer. "Didn't you know me any better than that?"

She wasn't going to cry. *Please, God, don't let me cry.* "At that point, I didn't know anything except that what I had once hoped for was now completely out of reach. I had a child on the way. A child I didn't want."

"There were options," he told her quietly. Not options that he would have chosen for her, but they were hers to reject, not his.

She shook her head. "Not for me."

"Then adoption," he suggested.

Lilli shook her head. "My mistake, my burden," she said firmly.

Her reasoning frustrated him. His anger against the dead man bubbled up within him and he had nowhere to vent it. His temper flared and it was a struggle to keep it under wraps. "He raped you, you didn't rape him. How the hell was any of this your mistake?" he asked.

She'd told him what he needed to know. She didn't want to talk about it anymore.

She waved away his question. "That's all in the past. And in one of those ironic twists of fate, Jonathan is the best thing that ever happened to me." Pausing, she looked at him, then softly amended, "Well, one of the best."

She could sense that he wanted to ask more questions. Lilli looked down at her hands. She'd just stripped herself naked and felt utterly vulnerable.

"Satisfied?" she asked in a whisper.

Chapter Seven

Sympathy, guilt and anger suddenly warred within Kullen.

The sympathy was self-explanatory. The guilt was because he'd had to force her to relive the ordeal, and the anger was directed against the narcissistic bastard who'd assaulted Lilli. And ultimately robbed them of a life they could have had together.

"No, I'm not," he told her. "I won't be satisfied until I can beat Erik Dalton within an inch of his life."

"But he's dead."

"Hence, my dilemma," Kullen acknowledged with a straight face.

It took her a second to realize he was kidding. Lilli laughed softly. "You always did know how to make me smile."

"We do what we can," he quipped with affection.

He kept it light. What he really wanted to say was

that she should have come to him with this the moment she knew she was pregnant. It pained him to think of her facing something so huge on her own. He would have been there for her every step of the way if only he'd known. If only she'd trusted him to stand by her and not judge her.

But for now he kept the question to himself. He could see that Lilli just wanted to table the subject. He had no choice but to abide by her obvious wishes.

In his mind, Kullen promised himself that they would come back to this discussion in the near future. Lilli needed to fully purge herself of this incident. She'd taken the first important steps. The rest would come.

"Do you think she can do it?" Lilli asked, trying her best to disguise the tremor in her voice. "Do you think that Mrs. Dalton will be able to take Jonathan away from me?"

He chose his words carefully, his eyes never leaving hers. "I think Elizabeth Dalton's going to do her damnedest to try," he told her, "but no, I don't think she's going to take your son away from you."

Her hand covered his, creating the bond that she so desperately needed. "Promise?"

Logically, Kullen knew he couldn't guarantee anything. It was no secret that judges were a whimsical breed. If he and Lilli drew the wrong judge for the case, one who was either impressed by Elizabeth Dalton or whose appointment had somehow been facilitated by her pull or covert financial backing, then they were in for a hard fight—and the daunting possibility of an initial ruling against them.

But he knew that Lilli wasn't asking him for a logical

answer, or the truth when it came down to that. She was asking him for an answer that she could hang on to with both hands. An answer that told her everything would be all right. What she needed most of all was hope.

After all she'd been through, he figured it was the least he could do. So he smiled at her and said the one word she wanted to hear. "Promise."

The sigh that escaped her lips was one of relief and she mirrored his smile. But her expression told him she knew what he was doing and why. She appeared grateful that, for her sake, he was playing the game. There was time enough to deal with reality and all its hoary ramifications later.

"Thank you," she told him with feeling. "And now, I'd better get back and tell my mother she's free to go home if she wants to. Although half the time I suspect she likes sticking around Jonathan and me. Now that my dad's gone, we're all the family she has."

It occurred to him that he hadn't given her condolences where they were due. "I'm sorry to hear about your dad."

"Yeah, me, too." Her father had died shortly after Jonathan was born. Because she'd been in the midst of dealing with her own issues, she hadn't known of his sudden illness until a week before he passed away. She blamed herself for that, too, and still grieved that her father never got to see his grandson.

Wanting to change the subject, Kullen nodded toward the pizza box. There was still a little less than half left.

"Why don't you take some of this with you for Jonathan?" he suggested. He saw that she was about to demur—he could still read so much of her body language. Funny how some things never left you, he thought. "I don't know of any seven-year-old boy alive who doesn't like cold pizza." With that, he went to the kitchen to get a container for her.

Lilli followed him. "Don't you want it?"

"I've got more than enough," he assured her. "Just in case you didn't notice, you still eat like a bird on a diet."

Kullen opened an overhead cupboard and she saw a collection of plastic containers of all sizes and shapes crowded together. She couldn't help wondering if they would all wind up raining down if he attempted to take one out.

"New hobby of yours?" she asked, nodding toward the containers.

He laughed. "My mother thinks I'm going to starve to death. She makes it a habit of dropping off what she calls leftovers from her catering business about once every week or so. I keep meaning to give these back to her."

Carefully extracting a rectangular container and its lid, he managed not to upset the rest of the pyramid. Apparently, Lilli mused, the man had added magic tricks to his skills since she'd last seen him. She followed him back to the dining room.

Opening the container, Kullen put two slices of pizza into it. He saw a quizzical look enter her eyes. "One for your mother, in case she's built up an appetite running after your son."

Her smile widened. "She doesn't chase him around. Jonathan is extremely well behaved. Not an ounce of trouble, ever." She was aware of the note of pride in her voice.

"Like his mother," Kullen commented. Taking the container with him, he walked her to the door, then handed it to her just as he opened the door for her.

She turned in the doorway and looked up at him. "Thank you again," she said with feeling. "For everything."

He knew she meant for understanding and for not pushing the matter. What good would it have done to verbally pin her against the wall? Berating her would have made neither one of them feel any better.

Leaning over, he brushed his lips ever so lightly against her forehead. It was what a big brother might have done with a sister. Though he longed to really kiss her, he had a feeling that it would really spook her.

Just like old times, Kullen couldn't help thinking. After all these years, this had the familiar feeling of square one. "It's included in my fee," he told her glibly.

The fee. She knew his services didn't come cheaply and she was not about to impose on him because of their past friendship. He'd mentioned taking her on pro bono but that wasn't what she wanted. She paid her own way, no matter how long it took.

"About that—"

He knew without asking that she didn't have the kind of money this case would cost. He would have to figure something out. If push came to shove, he could cover the expenses out of his own pocket. Barring that, he could possibly do a little string pulling if need be to satisfy the senior partners. And there was always pro bono to fall back on as a last resort. He didn't want her to have to worry about money on top of everything else.

"We'll work it out," he promised her, cavalierly dismissing the subject.

The look of gratitude in her eyes had no price tag. "You're a godsend."

"Yeah, that's me," he cracked. "A gift from God."

Impulsively, she kissed him on the cheek and then hurried away to her car, parked at the curb right in front of his house. He stood in the doorway, watching her as she unlocked the door on the driver's side. She waved at him just before she got in.

Waving back, Kullen followed her with his eyes until she'd driven down the block and turned the corner, disappearing out of sight.

He stood there a little while longer. Absently, his fingers traced the very real imprint of her lips against his cheek. The phrase about not being able to go home again echoed in his head.

Leaning against the doorjamb, Kullen took a deep breath and straightened up. He was going to regret this, he thought. No matter how altruistic his motives might be, he was opening himself up for a world of hurt and he knew it.

Turning on his heel, he went inside and closed the front door. Wishing he could close off everything else just as easily.

"So you were serious this afternoon? About taking on a case as a favor for an old flame?"

He'd stepped outside for a moment to throw what was now an empty pizza box into his recycle bin. When he came back inside, it was to the insistent sound of a ringing phone. Kullen managed to snatch up the receiver just as he heard his answering machine start to pick up. His intervention terminated the action.

Kate was on the other end of the line. She certainly didn't waste any time, he thought.

Suddenly thirsty, he caught himself wishing for a beer. With the receiver nestled against his shoulder and his neck, he opened the refrigerator. He had a hunch that no matter how much he stared into the interior, a bottle or can of beer would *not* materialize.

"How come, all those years we lived at home together, you never told me you thought you were a psychic?" His voice grew more serious. He hadn't told her that he'd had any sort of relationship with Lilli. There was no reason for her to believe that it was anything but fleeting, the way all his relationships had been these last seven years. "Who told you she was an old flame?"

He heard her chuckle and suddenly knew he'd walked into a setup. "You just did, big brother. Although I have to admit that Selma started the ball rolling this afternoon by saying that you looked a little off your game with the new client."

He knew how she operated. "And being the insatiably curious person that you are, you had to know why and you started digging."

"Like a little ferret," she informed him. "Especially when I wheedled your client's name out of Selma. You do remember that Mom sent this woman over, right? It's her way of playing matchmaker with you."

Yes, he knew, but it didn't matter how Lilli got here as long as she did. Closing the refrigerator door again, he straddled the kitchen chair he'd pulled over. "Don't you have anything better to do with your time? Isn't your caseload big enough?"

"Fortunately for you, I'm very fast as well as very thorough." She got down to business. "I'm calling you to offer my services." When there was only silence on the line, she prodded a little. "You know, do some research, find the right references. Off the books, of course," she was quick to add. "This way, Rothchild won't get his shorts in a twist. After all, he won't be pleased when he hears you're going up against Elizabeth Dalton, she of the Dalton Pharmaceuticals fortune."

Kullen sighed. "Is there anything you don't know?" he asked.

"You mean about how much your old flame meant to you and how cut up you were when she disappeared?"

"Who—?"

"Gil told me. And before you go blaming him after all these years, he told me because at the time he was worried about you. I just didn't make the connection when you mentioned a new client earlier."

"And telling my little sister about this so-called flame was going to help?" he asked, annoyed with Gil, a friend he had since lost touch with through no fault of his own.

"Eventually," she said loftily. "See, I'm offering to help you now. Don't look a gift horse in the mouth, Kullen," she advised playfully.

He laughed shortly. "I'd hardly call you a gift, but there is something you can do for me."

"Charming as always," she quipped. "Okay, what is this thing I can do for you?"

His answer surprised her. "Get me Jewel's phone number."

Jewel and Nikki were both her best friends and they went way back. They were also, all three of them, victims of their mothers' matchmaking endeavors. "She's spoken for, remember?" she deadpanned.

"I remember, wise guy. And that's not why I want to talk to her. I want Jewel to do a little investigating for me. Off the record," he added.

"Of course. Jewel'll be thrilled."

"I don't need her to be thrilled, I just need her to be thorough," he told Kate.

"Then you're in luck. Thorough just happens to be Jewel's middle name. Hold on a sec." He heard Kate putting the phone down and then shuffling in the background. His sister was back on the line a couple of minutes later. "Got a piece of paper and a pencil?" Without waiting for him to answer, she rattled off the number for the cell phone that Jewel used on the job.

Kullen thanked her and just as she was about to hang up, he stopped her. He had to ask. It wasn't that he and Kate had the kind of relationship where they were at odds all the time. For the most part, they got along fairly well. But this was definitely tendered out of the blue and he considered it over and above the call of duty on her part.

"Why are you doing this?" he asked. "Why are you volunteering like this?"

Her answer was flippant. "I need a few more points to get my merit badge in sainthood. I figured this would put me over the top. And because maybe I want to see you get a slice of happiness, too."

Perhaps there was a little bit of their mother in Kate as well, he thought. This was the new Kate. The old one would have never given the green light to a setup, even if it didn't involve her. She only had the best of intentions, as did their mother. But he had a feeling he would wind up paying for this. "If you're talking about Lilli and me, that was a long time ago."

"But not in a galaxy far, far away," she pointed out glibly.

He laughed, shaking his head. It was official. Love had made his sister crazy. "You realize that you need serious help, don't you?"

"No, but you might," she countered. The next moment, her voice softened as she continued. "I just wanted you to know that you're not alone in this."

There was no *this*. There was only a case that involved someone he'd once thought he knew. Someone who needed the kind of help he could provide. "Kate—"

"Yes?" she asked innocently.

He was about to tell her that he'd changed his mind and didn't need any help from her, but that would have been a lie. He backed off. They'd had the same sort of rivalry that most brothers and sisters had, and, like most siblings, at bottom was a strong foundation of love. He could count on her as much as she could count on him.

"Thanks," he finally said.

He could hear her smile through the phone. "Don't mention it. And good luck," she added, saying, "I never did like that Dalton woman."

"When did you ever have any dealings with her?"

"I didn't, outside of the society page," Kate confessed.

"But there's just something about the way she comes across, that strong sense of superiority she always radiates. She's a snob who thinks that she's entitled to anything she wants just because she wants it. People like that *really* annoy me." She abruptly interrupted herself. "Uh-oh, got a call coming in on the other line. Hopefully, it's Jackson," she said, referring to her fiancé. "Gotta go. Let me know what I can do to help," she said. The next moment, the line had gone dead.

Keeping her number in front of him, Kullen lost no time calling Jewel. She was surprised to hear from him. Surprised and pleased when he told her why he was calling.

"I just wrapped up a case," she told him cheerfully, "and was wondering what I was going to do with myself in the spare seven minutes I had before I get to start the next one."

Kullen put his own interpretation on her words. "If you're too busy, Jewel—" he began. He was willing to go with a referral from her, although he wasn't a hundred percent comfortable about it. He knew Jewel always went the extra mile.

She cut him off before he got any further. "Hey, you're Kate's big brother. I'm not too busy, even if I am."

He supposed, in an odd way, that made sense to him. "Easy to see why you and Kate get along so well. You both talk the same kind of double-talk."

"And don't you forget it," Jewel laughed with pride. And then she got down to business. "Okay, what do you need?"

He'd give her the particulars when he saw her. Right

now he just offered an overview. "In a nutshell, I need you to find out if there are any skeletons in Elizabeth Dalton's closet that we could use in case we need to keep her in line."

"Elizabeth Dalton," Jewel repeated. "As in *rich* Elizabeth Dalton?" she asked, then further qualified, "As in Dalton Pharmaceuticals?"

He hadn't thought that Elizabeth Dalton was that common a name. Obviously, he'd thought wrong. "Yes and yes."

He heard her give a low whistle. Jewel was either impressed or intimidated. Since she was one of his sister's two lifelong best friends, he was pretty certain that it was the former. Kate didn't suffer cowards very well and would have never hung around with someone who was fearful.

Still there might have been other reasons for her reaction to the name. "Problem?" he asked.

"No, no problem. But I am curious. Why do you need someone to go digging through her past?"

"Her late son, Erik, fathered a child."

"Only one?" she marveled. "The way I read that he was going before his accident, I assumed he got a lot of mileage out of his rich status. There should be little Eriks scattered through the Southwest."

Jewel had a point, he thought. They should look into other paternity issues. "Right now, only one that we know of. Mama Dalton wants custody of the boy. The boy's mother doesn't want to give him up."

"And you've taken up the mother's cause."

He brushed aside any discussion of his motives. "Something like that. If you come by the office tomorrow, I can give you all the particulars." He knew it sounded as if he was taking her for granted, so he asked, "Are you interested?"

"Absolutely." Her enthusiasm was impossible to miss. "It's been a while since I had a really interesting case. Nice to be able to exercise my brain cells for a change, instead of just using my telephoto lens and snapping men with their pants down."

"Be careful who you say that around," he warned with a laugh. "Your fiancé might not be too understanding about that."

"My fiancé is fantastic, but thanks for worrying," she said cheerfully. "Two o'clock okay with you?"

He'd settle for two if he had to, but it wasn't his first choice. "Earlier if you can make it."

Jewel never hesitated. "Earlier it is. Nine early enough for you?"

"Perfect."

Her laugh was low and throaty. "So I've been told," Jewel said just before she hung up.

He replaced the receiver.

Okay, he thought, everything was in motion and he was committed. No turning back now.

Kullen rolled up his sleeves and got to work.

Chapter Eight

There was wealth and then there was *wealth*, Kullen decided as he caught his first glimpse of the thirty-room mansion where Elizabeth Dalton resided. It was one of five such houses, for lack of a better word, that she owned.

He took it all in as he slowly drove up the winding, light blue-gray paved driveway. Comprised of carefully chosen pavers, the path appeared far more pristine than his own kitchen floor after his once-a-month cleaning service got through with it.

Elizabeth Dalton could qualify as her own self-contained country, keeping an army of people employed. Someone not only maintained the vast grounds but obviously cleaned them as well. Diligently.

He brought his sedan to a stop beside an impressive marble fountain. A sculpture of Neptune, water shooting from his trident, caught Kullen's attention. The fountain stood several yards before a building that could not, by any stretch of the imagination, be referred to as a home. The word *compound* came to mind. Especially when a smartly uniformed young man unobtrusively emerged from the side to inform him that he would be parking the car. The apparition put his hand out for the keys.

Getting out, Kullen eyed the man uncertainly. Apparently Elizabeth Dalton had her own valet. Nobody should be that rich.

"It'll be waiting for you when you come out, sir," the valet assured him as he continued holding his hand out, waiting for the keys.

Kullen was neither accustomed to this kind of service when paying a courtesy call to an opposing client, nor to being addressed as "sir" by someone roughly his own age. Possibly older. There was something uncomfortable about both situations.

But, in the interest of being cooperative, he nodded and surrendered his key.

Getting in behind the wheel, the valet told him, "Terrence will take you to Mrs. Dalton."

"Terrence," Kullen muttered under his breath, turning toward the mansion's front door. "Who the hell is Terrence?"

Terrence, it turned out, was the man who opened the door when Kullen rang the bell. Actually, he reconsidered as it continued pealing, *bell* was a paltry word in this case. Cathedral chimes was a more appropriate description of the sound that resulted from a simple press of his forefinger.

The woman certainly knew how to be intimidating—too bad it was all lost on him, Kullen thought, looking around and taking it all in as he was led into the ornate foyer. He'd grown up living in the same house with his father who had, in his own way, turned intimidating into an art form. Anthony Manetti had done it out of love, his mother had maintained. Being so strict was just his way of getting the very best out of his people and his children.

Kullen had never appreciated the lesson until just now. It prepared him for meeting the likes of Elizabeth Warfield Dalton.

"Mrs. Dalton is waiting for you in the library," the tall, thin man who had introduced himself as Terrence informed him, leading the way to one side of the building.

Kullen could have sworn that the hike from the door to the so-called library—did people actually *have* libraries these days?—was close to a half mile.

He should have brought breadcrumbs. Either that, or a pocket GPS to help him find the front door when the time came.

At the end of a journey filled with twists and turns was Elizabeth Dalton. She sat on a sofa, her face turned toward the door. A regal, attractive auburn-haired woman, she had the carriage of a queen. Kullen had a feeling that he was in danger of hearing her shout, "Off with his head!" if he displeased her.

"Mr. Manetti, you came," Elizabeth said in a firm, confident voice.

She Who Must Be Obeyed, he thought, recalling the title of an old science fiction movie he'd once caught on a cable channel.

Leaning forward, Elizabeth extended her hand to him.

Kullen wasn't sure if she was waiting for him to shake it or kiss it. Exercising his free will, he chose the former.

"I doubted if I had a choice," he replied amiably. "I've never been summoned before."

The tight smile on her small, perfect lips never wavered. "I'm sure you have," she contradicted knowingly. "You see, I knew your father."

"Apart from that," he amended.

"Please, sit," she coaxed, one perfectly manicured hand patting the seat beside her.

As he sat down, Kullen braced himself for absolutely anything.

"It's a very nice palace you have here," he quipped.

She smiled magnanimously, allowing him the one parry. "It's home."

No, Buckingham Palace is home, he thought. *This amounts to an entire city.*

Sitting back, Elizabeth never took her eyes off him. Obviously, the woman subscribed to the theory that it was good to keep the enemy in your sights at all times.

"I won't waste your time, Mr. Manetti. I asked you here so that we could arrive at some kind of satisfactory arrangement." Elizabeth inclined her stylishly coiffured head whimsically. "A deal, I believe you might call it."

So this was an out-of-court negotiation. He hadn't expected one so soon. He'd only been the attorney on record for a few days. The woman worked fast. But something was off. Kullen looked around. "Shouldn't one of your lawyers be here for this?"

The smile never reached her eyes. "I thought it better this way since the arrangement I'm proposing would be strictly between the two of us."

"You and my client," he asked, seeking to clarify just who she was referring to. He had an uneasy feeling that it wasn't the two he cited.

And he was right.

The smile on Elizabeth's lips turned positively reptilian to him.

"No, Mr. Manetti, between you and myself. You're a bright young man with an equally bright future before you. I can make it better, infinitely better. I can supply you with connections you never dreamed possible, introduce you to a world beyond your wildest imagination."

In a nutshell, she was asking him to sell his soul. "And all I have to do is sell out my client," he concluded, showing no emotion.

She frowned slightly, then reined in her annoyance. The smile appeared more forced than before. "That's such a harsh description. I don't want you to sell out. I want you to make her see reason." She gestured about, taking in not only the house but her vast holdings as well. "I can offer my grandson the world. She has nothing to compare with that."

His eyes met hers. "A mother's love."

Elizabeth Dalton began to laugh, as if he was sharing a simpleminded joke with her. And then she stopped, her eyes widening as she looked at him, the truth dawning on her. "Oh, my God, you actually believe that, don't you?"

He wasn't about to allow her ridicule to undermine him. Moreover, he began to see why Erik Dalton had been such an ass.

"Yes, I do."

Still seated, she drew herself up as if to cast a formidable shadow. "Then we have nothing else to talk about."

"It doesn't look that way, no," he agreed, glad and relieved to be leaving this poisonous woman's company. "I'd say it was a pleasure, Mrs. Dalton, but that same man who used to summon me also taught me not to lie."

With that, he turned his back on her and began to walk out of the room.

"You can't win, you know," Elizabeth called after him as he crossed the threshold.

Kullen didn't bother turning back around to face her. But he did toss off a reply as he continued on his way out of her lair. "We'll see."

He thought he heard the woman utter a curse in response, but he wasn't sure. All he wanted to do was get out of there.

On the way back to Orange County, Kullen struggled to get his temper under wraps and back on an even keel. Elizabeth Dalton obviously thought she had the right to play God with people's lives. It took him the better part of twenty miles to get himself under control.

Since he'd signed himself out of the office before

he'd left to see Mrs. Dalton, he was free to go home. He thought of stopping for a beer.

Or three.

But then he'd have to wait several hours before he was able to drive home and that held no appeal for him. But he did want some company and at least one beer, if not more.

As he got off the 405 freeway, a convenience store caught his attention. He pulled up to it and picked up a six-pack of his favorite brand of amber refreshment, and a couple of other items as well.

He decided to drop by Lilli's place and give her an update. He wanted to tell her about the command performance before Elizabeth Dalton, the Red Queen, beat him to it and called Lilli herself, twisting facts to suit her purposes. The woman was capable of a great many things that didn't come under the heading of Love Thy Neighbor.

He wanted to assure Lilli that if he'd harbored any doubts about going to the mat with this case, those doubts were now completely and permanently emulsified. Elizabeth Dalton had seen to that.

And then he wanted to ask Lilli how she had refrained from punching the woman out when Mrs. Dalton had initially made the offer to, in effect, "buy" Lilli's son and take him from her. One woman could hit another woman, whereupon a man could not.

Rules could be very annoying.

By the time he finally pulled up in front of Lilli's house, twilight tip-toed. He sat in his car for a moment, wondering if he would disturb her by coming over unannounced like this. And while he sat, debating, it struck him how much more real this small, tidy two-story house was than the one that Elizabeth Dalton rattled around in.

Taking a breath, he picked up the bag of goods he'd bought at the convenience store and got out of the car.

It had been one of those days when she felt she was going ninety miles an hour while everyone else was going a hundred and ten. With an incredible number of tasks to accomplish, Lilli was falling behind and she hated that.

Rochelle, one of the two salesgirls who worked for her at the boutique she managed, had called in sick this morning. The other salesgirl, a cheerful little thing named Judy, had left the shop early to pick up relatives flying in from Phoenix.

That left only Lilli to handle the customers *and* the inventory. The latter needed to be completed by the end of the week if she had any hopes of placing a timely order with the shop's suppliers. If the order didn't go through, there would be empty shelves and empty hangers on the racks next month, which the owner of the shop wouldn't appreciate.

Days like today made her feel as if she were holding on by the tips of her fingers. And coming perilously close to losing her grip and falling down into the abyss.

All she really wanted to do was stay home with her son and close the door to keep the rest of the world from barging in. But if she gave in to that overwhelming desire, her carefully constructed world would fall apart around them.

It still might, but she chased that thought away.

Shorthanded, she'd been late getting home. She knew that her mother, bless her, was always there to pick up the slack, but she desperately needed some alone time with her son. Desperately needed to unwind and pretend, just for a little while, that everything was all right and would continue to be that way.

Her mother had left fewer than ten minutes ago. Because of her, dinner was waiting for them on the stove and Jonathan had finished his homework.

The woman was a saint, Lilli thought, kicking off her shoes and getting comfortable. She had no idea what she would do without her. The idea of leaving Jonathan with a stranger now left her cold.

Walking into the kitchen, Lilli glanced toward the stove. Her mother had made a large chicken pot pie—the healthy kind, her mother had stressed—and it smelled wonderful. But Lilli had no appetite. Worry, no matter how hard she tried to keep it at bay, had a habit of wearing a hole in her stomach. Her only incentive to sit down at the table to eat was if Jonathan hadn't had dinner yet, either. But her mother was good about things like that. She made sure that Jonathan ate at the same time every night because a sense of stability was important for a child.

After greeting Lilli with the small, fierce hug she'd come to need more than the very air she breathed, Jonathan had run off to the family room to play his new video game. Maybe she could get something down if she took her dinner to the family room and watched him play.

About to spoon out a small serving of the pot pie, Lilli heard the doorbell ring. Her first thought was that her mother had forgotten something. But then she realized in the next moment that her mother wouldn't ring the doorbell. She had a key to the front door.

Who—

"I'll get it!" Jonathan called out.

Lilli's heart froze, then dropped like lead into the pit of her already knotted stomach.

"No!" she cried.

Her sudden onset of fear didn't arise from the general rule that every mother tried to impress upon her children not to open the door to strangers. There was a far greater danger to deal with than that. What if for some reason the person on the other side of the door was Elizabeth? Or one of myriad people who worked for her? What if they were here for Jonathan? How long did it take to whisk a small boy away? One, two seconds? Three, tops?

Dropping the silverware she'd just taken from the drawer, Lilli didn't even hear it clatter to the tile floor as she ran out of the kitchen.

"Don't open the door, Jonathan!" she shouted to her son.

But it was too late. Jonathan had already pulled it open.

"Hi," he guilelessly greeted the person standing on his doorstep.

With hair like golden wheat and bright blue eyes, the boy looked like a miniature version of Lilli, Kullen thought. He smiled like his mother, too.

"Hi," Kullen said, grinning down at the boy. "You must be Jonathan."

"I am," the boy confirmed solemnly.

"Is your mother home?" The words were barely out of his mouth when the door was pulled open all the way. A breathless, frightened looking Lilli filled the newly created space. "I guess you are," he quipped.

When she saw that it was Kullen and not anyone associated with Mrs. Dalton, Lilli breathed a huge sigh of relief.

"Oh, thank God, it's you."

Kullen laughed. "I've definitely had worse greetings." And then he sobered just a little. "Is something wrong?"

Her attention shifted to her son. "Yes, something's wrong." They'd talked about this more than once. "What did I tell you about opening the door?"

"Don't," the boy parroted solemnly.

It was impossible to be angry with him. He was the light of her life. But still, she needed him to understand that he couldn't yank open the door whenever he heard someone knocking. There could be serious consequences. She could only keep him safe as long as he was within her reach.

"So why did you?" she wanted to know.

His expression was innocence personified. And genuine. "I just wanted to help you, Mom. You were busy in the kitchen."

"Can't argue with altruism like that," Kullen told her. He nodded at the interior of her home, so much smaller than Elizabeth Dalton's. So much warmer. "Can I come in?"

Coming to, Lilli stepped back. "Of course. And as for arguing with altruism, I most certainly can." She looked at Kullen. "What if it hadn't been you ringing the bell? What if it was one of Mrs. Dalton's people?" She lowered her voice so that her son couldn't hear. "They could have kidnapped him in the time it took me to reach the door."

Following her in, Kullen stopped short. "Is that really a concern?" he asked seriously.

The look on Lilli's face told him far better than any words that it was.

Because this was someone new, Jonathan was hanging around instead of running back to his game. She turned away so that her son couldn't hear.

"I don't know what she's capable of or what her limits are," Lilli told him in a whisper. "Or even if she has any."

"Well, one thing I can tell you is that her limits don't exclude bribery," Kullen said.

It was her turn to stop dead in her tracks. He thought he saw her pale. "What do you mean?"

Removing it from a brown paper bag, he held up the six-pack of beer he'd brought over. "I'll tell you over a can of beer."

The boy looked excited. "Can I have a beer, too?" Jonathan asked.

"No," Lilli said automatically. Her voice blended with Kullen's, except that to her surprise he'd said yes. She stared at him, dumbfounded. "Yes?" she questioned. Was he out of his mind? You didn't give beer to a child. Ever.

Kullen took out one of the cans of soda he'd thought to buy. "I brought him some root beer," he said, explaining. "I didn't want him to feel left out."

She felt her heart melting. She'd forgotten how sweet

Kullen could be. For a second, she fervently wished that she could go back, do things over. But there were no "do-overs" in life. It was what it was and she'd plotted her course a long time ago.

Smiling at him, she said, "That was very thoughtful of you."

Kullen shrugged off the compliment and handed the soda to Jonathan, who puffed up his chest as if he thought he'd officially become one of the big boys. "I'll get the glasses," he volunteered, dashing into the kitchen ahead of them.

The clinking of glasses was heard. Lilli refrained from taking over and bringing thc glasses to the table. She knew she needed to encourage every spark of independence, no matter how hard it was on her. Or, in this case, the glasses.

"Mrs. Dalton sent for me," Kullen told her as they sat down at the table.

"Sent?" she asked as Jonathan handed out the glasses and then climbed up on a chair.

"Actually," Kullen reflected, "*summoned* would be a better word." Popping a top, he slowly poured beer into a tall glass the boy had placed before him. Out of the corner of his eye, he saw Jonathan mimicking his actions.

"She *summoned* you?" Lilli echoed in disbelief. "Why?"

Leaning over, Kullen opened her beer for her and then poured it. "I believe she thought the bribe would sound more impressive if I saw the size of her estate first."

"Mrs. Dalton tried to bribe you?" she asked gently. "With what, money?"

"With my future, actually." He took a sip, letting it slide down before he continued. "She said that she knew a great many influential people who could do a lot for me." He laughed shortly, shaking his head at what a small world it could be at times. "Turns out she knew my father, too."

Every sound around her—the hum of the refrigerator, Jonathan sipping his soda—was magnified. Lilli could hardly draw a breath. She knew the allure of what the other woman was offering, knew she had no right to ask him to turn his back on something so beneficial to his career.

But if Kullen withdrew from her case, she wouldn't have time to find anyone else. And who was to say that anyone else would be immune to what the woman could offer.

"What did you say to her?" she asked in a small, still voice.

He grinned and suddenly she felt as if there was hope. "Not in front of the boy."

"You turned her down?" Lilli cried hopefully.

He looked at her for a moment, stunned that she would be so surprised. "Of course I turned her down. You really don't know me at all, do you?"

A feeling of weariness came over her. "I don't really even know myself anymore," she confessed.

He made it easy for her. "Okay, you're a work in progress. I'm not." Placing the glass back on the table, he spread out his hands for her benefit. "What you see, Lilli, is what you get."

I should have trusted you back then, Kullen. I should have.

Out loud, she told him, "Then I'm getting quite a lot."

Chapter Nine

Not quite sure how to respond to the comment Lilli had just made, Kullen turned toward the boy on his left. "How's your 'beer,' champ?" he asked Jonathan.

Obviously pleased to be included and noticed by his mother's friend, the boy grinned broadly. "Great!" To prove it, he took another long sip from his glass.

Kullen struggled not to laugh at Jonathan's enthusiasm. He didn't want to hurt the boy's pride. "I'm glad to hear that."

Jonathan shifted about in his seat, unable to sit still. Lilli couldn't remember ever seeing him like this. Normally, he was a sedate, quiet boy. But then, there were only women in his world. Her mother, his teacher. Her. He was far more alive around Kullen. He needed male influence, and she was grateful to Kullen for treating her son like a person who mattered.

"Do you like video games?" Jonathan asked Kullen

suddenly, his eyes bright with hope. "I've got a good one I've been playing. Do you wanna see it?"

She didn't want Kullen to feel obligated to spend time with the boy. He'd already done enough. "Jonathan, Mr. Manetti doesn't have time for a video game."

Kullen winked conspiratorially at the boy, then said, "I don't mean to contradict your mom, but it just so happens that I do." He rose to his feet. "Lead the way," he told Jonathan, then looked over his shoulder at Lilli. "You can come, too, 'Mom.' Unless you brought home-work to do."

She had, but it wasn't nearly as appealing as watch-ing Kullen interact with her son. The inventory sheets could be postponed until later tonight. This was one of those moments you were supposed to stop and enjoy. And she fully intended to.

"It'll keep," Lilli said dismissively. Suddenly feeling her appetite coming to life, she glanced back at the stove. "I was just about to have some pot pie my mother made. Would you like some?"

He hadn't had any dinner yet. Without missing a beat, he told her with boyish enthusiasm, "I'd love some." Not wanting to leave out Jonathan, he looked at him and asked, "How about you, champ? You hungry, too?"

Jonathan shook his head, his flaxen hair moving back and forth about his ears. "I ate dinner with Grandma," Jonathan told him.

Grinning, Kullen ruffled his hair. "Nice of you to keep your grandmother company. I'm sure she appreci-ated it."

Jonathan beamed at the approval. "Yeah, she's nice," the boy said with feeling. Rushing into the family room ahead of his new friend, Jonathan grabbed the box the video game had come in and held it up for Kullen's perusal. "I'm playing this one. But it'd be more fun if you played, too."

Lilli looked from the box to Kullen. Her expression was skeptical. "Do you know how to play video games?" she asked. She herself hadn't a clue, although she'd been meaning to learn for Jonathan's sake. But she knew right off the top that she just wasn't coordinated that way.

"Do I know how to play video games?" Kullen repeated with a laugh. The truth of it was, video games were his guilty pleasure. It was a way for him to unwind—when he wasn't spending time with his "flavor of the month," as Kate referred to the women who wove in and then out of his dating life. "Prepare to be dazzled," he promised Lilli as he sank down on the sofa next to her son.

For almost two hours, Kullen played with the aplomb and skill of someone who hadn't been a novice in a very long time. Lilli noticed that he held back just enough to allow her son to win the final round.

It warmed her heart to see Jonathan so enthralled and happy.

"Looks like you beat me, champ," Kullen marveled, putting down his controller on the coffee table. "But I'll get you next time," he promised with a wink.

"How about now?" the boy asked excitedly, picking up the controller and holding it out to him. He seemed ready to go at least another two hours.

Watching the so-called competition from the adjacent love seat, Lilli stepped in. "It's past your bedtime, Jonathan," she pointed out.

"Aw, Mom." He surprised her by whining in the sullen voice of little boys everywhere. "Just a few more minutes."

"It's going to take more than a few minutes to play this, champ," Kullen reminded him prudently. "Besides," he added, "I'm kind of beat. It's past my bedtime, too."

"You have a bedtime?" Jonathan marveled, half wide-eyed, half suspicious.

"All great video gamers have bedtimes," Kullen told him seriously. "Didn't you know that? We've got to get our rest so we can stay sharp. You never know when the next matchup is coming."

Suspicion faded. "Oh." Convinced, Jonathan bobbed his head. "Okay."

"You go on upstairs and get ready, sweetheart," Lilli instructed affectionately. "I'll be up in a few minutes to tuck you in."

"And to read me a story?" Jonathan added, eyeing her hopefully.

A story would take time. She didn't want to rush Kullen out and it wouldn't be polite to leave him standing around down here while she was upstairs, reading to her son.

"We'll see," she replied evasively.

Guessing at the source of her ambivalence, Kullen came to the rescue. "How about I read you a story?" Kullen proposed, looking at the boy.

Jonathan lit up like a Roman candle. "That'd be awesome!" he declared happily.

"Okay, you go upstairs and get ready for bed like your mom said and I'll be up there in a few minutes." Jonathan was already flying to the staircase. "Leave the door open so I can find your room," he called, cementing the bond he'd just forged with the boy.

"Yes, sir," the small boy all but crowed. He rushed up the stairs in record time.

"I never saw him move that fast before to get ready for bed," Lilli marveled. She turned toward Kullen, feeling her heart swell with warmth. "You know you didn't have to do any of that."

He shrugged, dismissing her gratitude. "I like playing video games. This gives me an excuse."

The video game was only part of it. "And picking up the cans of root beer?"

He shrugged again. "Just made sense at the time."

"All right, how about volunteering to read a story to him?"

Kullen laughed. That was no big deal. "Haven't you heard? Every lawyer likes to hear the sound of his or her own voice. Reading out loud fits right into that."

Lilli shook her head. The man was as unassuming as she remembered him. "Still can't take a compliment, can you?"

"When I deserve one," he countered. "But there's no reason to compliment me for doing something I enjoy." Looking at her, his expression grew serious. An uneasy feeling undulated through her. It didn't subside when she heard what he had to say. "Listen, we need to talk—"

"I'm ready, Mr. Kullen!" Jonathan called out, his voice drifting down the stairs.

"—but not now," Kullen concluded, doing a verbal

U-turn and tabling what he wanted to say to her for the time being.

She hadn't a clue what Kullen wanted to discuss with her and not knowing made her edgy. Exceedingly edgy. Her brain went into overdrive. Was Kullen being so incredibly nice to her son because he was trying to soften the blow?

Was he going to make a pitch for Mrs. Dalton's side after all? The very possibility numbed her.

No, she argued silently, he couldn't. He wouldn't. She *knew* him. She hadn't thought so, but she did. She *knew* him and the Kullen Manetti she knew wouldn't just set her up like this, wouldn't circle around her as if searching for her weak spot in order to attack her underside.

Dealing with Erik's mother these past few weeks had jaded her, had made her suspicious of everyone, seeing threats where none existed.

Damn, it isn't fair, she thought as she began to clean up the family room. She'd just started getting her life in order, just started trusting people again. Granted, she hadn't been out with a man on a date since before Jonathan was born—since she'd left Kullen, really—but that was because she wasn't interested in dating. The only man who was important in her life was still years away from shaving.

But she'd been able to relax a little more, had begun to feel at ease again. And then Mrs. Dalton had cornered her and first cajoled, then demanded custody of Jonathan. It was obvious that Elizabeth Dalton had expected nothing less than her total capitulation.

"Not used to anyone saying no to you, are you, you old viper?" Lilli muttered, wiping up the sweat ring

Kullen's beer can had left on the coffee table. "Well, I said no and I intend to keep on saying no until it sinks into that thick head of yours—or until I have to take Jonathan and go where you can never find either one of us."

Lilli stacked the two dishes she and Kullen had used, placed the glasses on top and carried them into the kitchen. She deposited everything in the sink.

"But you are never, never getting your claws into him, never changing him from the sweet boy he is into a carbon copy of his late father." Taking the cans next, she tossed them into a plastic garbage bag she used to stash recyclables. "For all I know, you did this to him," she theorized, back in the family room again. "Maybe Erik was as nice as Jonathan once but you turned him into that self-absorbed monster he became. That's not going to happen to my son."

"It won't."

Gasping even as she stifled a scream, Lilli swung around. Her body collided with Kullen's. He quickly grabbed her by the shoulders to keep her from falling. "Hey," he laughed, steadying her. "I'm not all *that* scary."

"You're not scary at all," she said once she caught her breath. "I just didn't hear you come up behind me and you startled me."

"Sorry, next time I'll call ahead," he promised with a wink. "I came down because I thought I heard you talking to someone."

She hadn't realized she'd been that loud. "Just to myself."

He appeared amused. "And did you agree with what you were saying?"

Lilli could feel herself withdrawing. "You're making fun of me."

"No," he contradicted. "I'm enjoying you. To be honest, hearing you mutter like that takes me back." She looked at him quizzically so he explained. "You used to talk to yourself when you were studying." Back then, the whole world lay before them. He'd thought she would accomplish wonderful things. "Why didn't you ever go back to school?"

She'd grown up rapidly that year, gone from being an idealistic student to the responsible mother of a child she hadn't initially wanted. But that part had changed the very first time she'd held Jonathan in her arms. "I couldn't. I had a baby to take care of."

Kullen pointed out the obvious. "Lots of lawyers have kids." As far as he was concerned, it was never too late to go back to school.

"Yes, but they usually have a spouse in the picture, someone ready to pitch in and pick up the slack at home."

That would have been me if you'd only trusted me enough to confide in me. Out loud he pointed out, "There was your mother."

But Lilli shook her head. "Not at first. When I left school, I went to live in Santa Barbara. I just moved back recently. I wanted my mother to get to know her grandson and I also thought I was going to need her support emotionally." She thought of the custody fight she was facing. "Right now, I can't devote myself to studying. Besides, I like managing the boutique." She'd mentioned that in one of their meetings, but had never said anything more about it.

"I've been meaning to ask you, what kind of a boutique is it that you manage?"

There was a fond smile on her lips. She'd made tactful suggestions since she'd been hired and had, in a very short time, left her own stamp on the shop.

"It's called Dreams," she told him. "We cater to the quiet woman who wants to break out of her shell, at least once. I recommend clothing, do makeovers—"

"And make dreams come true," he assumed, extrapolating from the shop's name.

A smile slipped into her eyes as she nodded. "Hence the name." It suddenly occurred to her that no one was upstairs with Jonathan. "What are you doing down here?" She began heading for the stairs. "Did you get tired of reading to your fan club?"

Moving quickly, Kullen got in front of her to prevent her going upstairs. "You don't have to go up to his room. Jonathan's asleep."

She stared at him, stunned. "You're kidding." She looked up the stairs, as if her gaze could penetrate walls and she could see her sleeping son for herself. "This has to be a first. Jonathan never goes to sleep in under an hour."

"Well, he's asleep," he assured her. "Must be the sound of my voice. Jonathan drifted right off by the time we got to page ten." Kullen grinned. "I was hoping he'd stay awake longer. I was kind of wondering what happened to the Indian."

"He asked you to read *The Indian in the Cupboard*?" This was a night for surprises, she thought. The book was set off to the side in what Jonathan called his "special place."

"Yes, why?"

"It's his favorite book. I'm the only one who's allowed to read that to him. Even my mother's not allowed to read it to him. He doesn't want anyone else touching the book. He's very fussy about that."

"Then I'm honored," he said and he was only half kidding.

You're more than that, she thought. *You're special to him.*

She'd never seen Jonathan take to anyone the way he had to Kullen. In literally minutes.

Like mother, like son.

She warned herself not to get too comfortable with this situation. With this man. She knew firsthand that things always fell apart just when they looked their best. And she had a feeling this would be no different.

But she needed to be and forced herself to focus on what counted. "You said before you went upstairs that you had something you wanted to discuss with me."

She saw Kullen's expression grow serious. "Ask you, actually."

An uneasiness undulated through her. Lilli had no idea what was coming but she braced herself for the worst. "Go ahead."

His eyes swept over her suddenly rigid countenance. Amused, Kullen asked, "Would you like a blindfold and a cigarette?"

"Excuse me?"

"No offense, but you look like you're getting ready to face a firing squad."

"Sorry, I've gotten into the habit of expecting the worst."

"Were you serious before, about being afraid that someone might try to kidnap Jonathan?" he asked.

She had been—and was—dead serious. "You probably think I'm paranoid."

He shook his head. He wasn't the one caught up in this. She would be the one who would know if there was a threat.

"Doesn't matter what I think. What matters is what you think. You're a lot closer to the situation than I am. Do you really think that there's a chance Mrs. Dalton would resort to having your son kidnapped?"

She took a breath. She didn't want him to think she was crazy, but she didn't want to lie or downplay this, either. "Honestly?"

"We won't get anywhere if you lie to me, Lilli, so yes, honestly."

"I think Elizabeth Dalton's given to obsessions. Right now, she's obsessed with getting my son. Maybe she thinks she can somehow make it up to Erik by raising his son. I do know that I said no to her and she doesn't tolerate being turned down very well."

She got down to his question. "I have nightmares that someone will break in and take Jonathan," she confessed. "I've been sleeping on the sofa lately so if anyone tries to break in, I'll hear them right away. I haven't slept through the night in weeks." Even as she said it, she stifled a yawn. "I keep thinking I hear things…." Her voice trailed off and she looked up at him. "You probably *do* think I'm paranoid. Or crazy. Or both."

"No, I don't think you're crazy. Or paranoid," he

assured her quietly. "I think you're a mother who's genuinely afraid of losing her son." And that, he knew, had to be a terrible situation.

He felt for her, for what she'd been going through, not just now, but for so long. Pausing, Kullen thought for a moment.

"Would it help if you had someone staying here with you?"

"You mean like a bodyguard?" she guessed. "I can't afford one, Kullen." And there was an additional problem. "Besides, what guarantee would I have that Mrs. Dalton wouldn't get to the bodyguard, make him an offer he couldn't refuse? Instead of having someone I could rely on to protect Jonathan, I would be, in effect, inviting the enemy into my house."

"It doesn't necessarily have to be that way," he told her.

"What do you mean?"

Kullen watched her eyes as he spoke. "What if your bodyguard was someone you knew?"

"Like who?"

Kullen smiled at her as he spread his hands wide, leaving himself open for her perusal. "Like me."

That would be a godsend, but it also wouldn't be fair to him. "I can't ask you—"

"You didn't," he cut in before she could protest. "I volunteered."

"Lawyer by day, bodyguard by night." She couldn't ask him to spread himself thin like that. "When would you sleep?"

"Why don't you let me worry about that?" he told her kindly.

Having him here at night would go a long way to calm her fears. She knew it was selfish of her, but the thought of having him here to keep Jonathan safe was too tempting to turn down more than once.

"Oh, God, Kullen," she cried, grateful beyond words. "You're being so good to me. I don't deserve it, not after the way—"

Kullen placed his finger against her lips to still them. "Again, why don't you let me worry about what you do or don't deserve?"

Lilli looked up at him, struggling to hold back tears.

There *weren't* any words to tell him how much what he was doing meant to her. She had only one method of communication, one way to let him know how very grateful she was to him.

Rising up on her toes, she placed her fingers softly about his face and kissed him.

He could taste her tears in the kiss.

Chapter Ten

Kullen never claimed to be a saint.

And if he'd become a great deal more experienced in sexual matters in the last eight years since Lilli had walked out of his life, it still hadn't prepared him for the intense longing now ricocheting throughout his entire body.

As the taste of her mouth registered, he felt like a man who had just been snatched back from the brink of starvation.

To be sure, he had the normal appetites of a man, but they were always coupled with the feeling that he could walk away from the situation, the frothy entanglement, at any time. While making love was an adrenaline-fueled undertaking, he would still be more than fine if they didn't go that route.

Everything was different with Lilli.

It always had been.

From the moment he'd met her, he had connected with her in a way he never had with any other woman since. Maybe that was because after Lilli had disappeared, he was careful to associate only with women who he didn't want to build a future with. Attractive women who enjoyed a good time and thrilled to the skills of an expert lover. But he made certain that there were never promises, never hints of a permanent foundation. Every woman he was with knew from the start that there was no future looming on the horizon. He engaged in light, breezy, good, clean, teeth-jarring sex.

But there was more in a single kiss from Lilli than from all the women he'd been with since put together. Though still holding himself in check, Kullen knew he was coming perilously close to throwing caution to the wind. To sweeping Lilli into his arms and kissing her the way he'd wanted to all these years. With his whole soul exposed.

The thought of revisiting soul-numbing heartache was a great deterrent. Kullen drew back, not a little mystified that he actually could.

He needed to put her on notice. "You do that again," he told Lilli quietly, "and you won't be able to hold me responsible for what happens."

Lilli trembled inside. She was both frightened and incredibly tempted, tempted to push the envelope just a little further. Tempted to kiss him again, but this time with even more feeling.

God, but she had missed him. Missed feeling safe because of him.

On the one hand, her life had no room for more complications. On the other, this was Kullen. Kullen, the man she should have been with all those years ago. The man she would have gladly married had life only arranged itself differently.

But it hadn't and she had made her peace with that. Made it over and over again. She had to work with what was, not with what might have been. The latter was pointless and only tortured her.

She'd been tortured enough.

But even so, she heard herself saying, "Maybe I don't want to hold you responsible."

Kullen took a deep, shaky breath, banking down a powerful surge of desire that threatened to break loose.

This is a test, right, God? he asked silently. And if he passed this test, nothing but emptiness waited for him on the other side. That was the prize, if it could be called that.

Emptiness.

Lilli was his client, he reminded himself. Lawyers who slept with their clients were seen as unethical. Everyone knew that. He had enough on his plate without opening himself up to disciplinary hearings.

Besides, if he wound up being taken to task for that and his license was temporarily suspended, who would fight for Lilli and her son?

Kullen put his hands on her shoulders and, rather than pull Lilli to him the way every fiber in his being longed to do, he gently pushed her back and held her there. Away from him.

"This would be a mistake right now, Lilli."

Taking a deep, fortifying breath, she nodded. "Right." At least one of them had common sense, she told herself.

But common sense was a poor substitute for a warm embrace. "If you're serious about staying here, I'll go get your bedding."

"I'm serious," he assured her. He'd made up his mind the moment she'd told him about her concern. He just hadn't realized when he'd made up his mind what a superhuman challenge it would be to keep his distance. "You need to get some rest."

Not with Kullen sleeping downstairs. Every cell in her body vibrated. It would take a long time before she would fall asleep—if at all. But at least she could rest easy knowing that Jonathan was safe.

Well, at least that made one of them, Lilli thought ruefully as she left the living room to get Kullen a pillow and blanket.

The feeling of being watched percolated through the layers of his brain, penetrating his consciousness before he was fully awake.

As sleep slowly ebbed from his haze-enshrouded brain, Kullen couldn't shake the uneasiness that someone was staring at him. *Really* staring at him.

Was he under surveillance?

Was there a spy camera somewhere on the premises, secretly planted by Mrs. Dalton's people in the hopes of gathering some kind of usable dirt on Jonathan's mother? Or were the cameras here just to let them know the best time to stage the kidnapping?

Or was this feeling simply a carryover from a dream he no longer could remember?

His eyes felt glued together. It occurred to his

awakening brain that he'd only fallen asleep a little while ago.

When he finally succeeded in forcing his eyelids apart, he discovered that there wasn't a tiny spy camera trained on him. Instead, it was a tiny spy. The eyes that stared at him so intently, as if to memorize every inch of him, belonged to the very person he was supposed to be keeping safe.

Jonathan.

The moment Kullen opened his eyes, Jonathan's intense look vanished, replaced by a huge grin.

"He's awake!" the boy announced at the top of his lungs, obviously sending a message of this new development to someone else in the house.

Hovering over him, their faces less than five inches apart, the seven-year-old turned his attention back to Kullen and guilelessly asked, "Are you going to live with us?"

Kullen sat up. He searched for a way to explain his presence, sleeping on the sofa, without unduly frightening the boy.

Walking into the living room, Lilli was just in time to come to his rescue—in more ways than one. "He's going to be staying here for a little while, Jonathan. You know, like a visitor." Pausing by the sofa, she handed Kullen a large mug of black coffee she'd just brewed for him. She served it with a smile. "Thought you might want this."

Given that his brain didn't kick in until he'd gotten the proper fuel, he more than wanted it, he *needed* it. "You're a lifesaver."

"Tit for tat," she answered glibly.

"What's a tat?" Jonathan asked, directing the question to either of the two adults before him who was able to answer. "And what's a ti—?"

Lilli quickly stopped him, placing her hand on his head before he could complete the question. "You have to get ready for school, young man. I have to get into work early this morning."

Jonathan seemed a little crestfallen. "Can't I stay home today with Mr. Kullen?"

"Sorry to disappoint you, champ, but I'm going to be going into work, too," Kullen told him.

"Oh." The boy thought it over for a moment and then his smile reappeared, lighting up his face. "Okay. I'll go get ready," Jonathan told his mother cheerfully, dashing out of the room.

Lilli sighed, watching her son race up the stairs. "God, but I wish I had half his energy."

"You're doing pretty well from where I'm sitting," Kullen assured her. After draining the last of his coffee, he put the mug on the coffee table and rose to his feet. "I'd better get home and change my clothes. I look like I slept in these."

"There's a reason for that," she laughed softly. "You did."

"True," Kullen conceded. "But I don't want Kate noticing if I can help it." When Lilli seemed puzzled, he explained, "She'll grill me."

"Oh, my money's on you. I'm sure you can hold your own against your sister," Lilli told him knowingly. "If you're interested, I made you breakfast. Blueberry waffles."

He was surprised by the choice. Blueberry waffles

were his favorite, but she'd have no way of knowing that. She didn't know what he ate for breakfast. There'd never been a morning after for them because there'd never been an evening before.

Just like there couldn't be now, he reminded himself. Morning and a night of sporadic sleep had done nothing to dampen the longing he'd experienced last night when she'd kissed him.

Just the mere memory sent lightning through his veins. He needed a cold shower. At home.

"I'll take that to go," he told her.

In an effort to save time, he followed her into the kitchen. She deftly deposited the waffles into a plastic container usually used to transport sandwiches and added a dollop of maple syrup before snapping on the lid. She tested it to make sure it held, then placed the container and a plastic fork into a paper bag for him.

He hadn't brown-bagged it since he'd been in school, Kullen recalled, feeling oddly pleased by the memory. Picking up his lunch, he promised her, "I'll be back tonight."

Lilli walked him to the front door. "I hate thinking that I'm putting you out this way."

"Then don't think about it," he countered, hesitating by the door. "You'll be all right if I leave now?" he asked.

She nodded. "Yes, thank you. It's only the nights that seem so foreboding." Lilli looked a little embarrassed. "I suppose that's being silly. But for some reason, I feel like I can hold my own and manage in the daylight."

She could hold her own in the darkness as well, Kullen couldn't help thinking. Forcing himself to focus only on the situation from a professional standing, he nodded at her. "I'll be back before sundown."

Knowing that he would made her feel infinitely better.

But at the same time, she felt guilty. She was taking advantage of his kind nature. "I don't want you to feel you *have* to be back."

He sighed, shaking his head. She hadn't changed. "You are the hardest woman to do something for, you know that? Stop protesting and just let me help you," he told her. "It'll go easier on both of us."

Her smile was shy and grateful and he could have spent hours getting lost in it. He would have to be very, very careful. "Okay."

Kullen left before he found another reason to stay.

His sedan was parked at the curb. When he looked back over his shoulder, just before he got into his car, Lilli was still standing there, framed in the doorway.

Just the way she was in his heart, Kullen suddenly realized.

This would be the most challenging case of his career to date.

The law—and Elizabeth Dalton with her expensive lawyers—had nothing to do with it.

"I stopped by your house last night."

A little more than an hour later, Kate walked into his office without bothering to knock. The way she looked at him, with his still damp hair, she must have figured that he'd had another one of his wild nights.

"You weren't there." Closing the door behind her,

she crossed to the leather sofa and perched on the edge. "But then, you already know that."

"I was working late," he countered evasively. "And I don't remember hearing you knock."

Her eyes held his. "Not here you weren't—and I didn't."

Ordinarily this would be the time when Kate would send a few zingers his way about the intellectual deficiency of the women he dated and bedded. That she didn't made him feel a little uncomfortable. Did she suspect something?

"I thought that Jewel was the one who did surveillance work," he said, deliberately sounding casual.

Kate dropped the flippant tone. "I'm not spying on you, Kullen," she told him. Getting up, she crossed to his desk. "This is me, being concerned."

Beneath her banter, he knew Kate only had his best interests at heart, but he didn't want her rummaging through his life, especially not now.

He curbed his natural impulse to tell her to butt out.

"Glad you cleared that up for me because I thought it was you, being nosy."

"That, too," Kate conceded, shrugging a shoulder carelessly. The corners of her mouth curved in a semi-smile. "But mostly, I was being concerned."

"Touching," he commented, searching through the piles of folders scattered about his desk. Where was the damn file he'd had out last night? He could have sworn he'd left it on the side of his desk. Someday, he would get a real filing system instead of relying on his memory.

"I'm being serious, Kullen." Leaning over his desk,

Kate lowered her face until it was level with her brother's. "Are you sure that you know what you're doing?"

"You mean taking on Elizabeth Dalton and her legion of shark lawyers?" He laughed shortly. "You know me, I love a challenge."

"Yes, I know, but I was talking about you getting back together with Lilli."

Kullen felt his back going up. Kate had just gone too far.

"For there to be a back together, there would have to have been an initial together somewhere in the past. And there wasn't." No matter how much he'd wanted it, he added silently. "Lilli and I were just law students at the same school, studying together. And then one day she just took off."

He did his best to sound distant, as if Lilli's leaving hadn't almost thrown him into a deep, dark pit. He thought he'd succeeded pulling this off rather well— until he looked into his sister's eyes.

He hadn't fooled her.

Kate's gaze pinned him against the wall. "I think there's more to it than that, big brother."

"You can think whatever you like." He looked away, focusing his attention on trying to locate the damn elusive file he needed. "That's why this is a free country."

She continued as if he hadn't all but come out and flatly told her to drop the subject.

"I think that Lilli's the reason you're so footloose and cavalier when it comes to your social life. You were different when you first went into law school. Mom and

I always thought you'd get married before you took your bar exam."

So did I. "Not me," Kullen told her glibly. "I like having my freedom, not being accountable to anyone. Now, if you don't mind." He gestured toward the door, his meaning abundantly clear. "I've got a lot of work to do today."

Kate straightened up but didn't move away from his desk. Not yet.

"I don't mind. I just thought you might want to use some of these court cases you had me hunting for. Custody battles between different generations of a family," she added in case he was drawing a blank.

That was when he first noticed that Kate held a slender file in her hand. She dropped it on his desk. He opened it and saw a list of cases with dates beside them. How had they ultimately turned out?

"What's the tally?" he asked.

"Fifty-fifty," she answered. "Sometimes the custody was awarded to the mother, sometimes not."

Kullen let the folder close and raised his eyes to hers. "Well, we're just going to have to change that," he said, more to himself than to her.

Kate smiled encouragingly. "If anyone can do that, it's you."

Kullen raised an eyebrow. "A compliment?" he queried. Kate was the one who usually came through with a stinging put-down. It was an ongoing game they played and he was as guilty as she of keeping it alive. "You're being nice to me?" he asked incredulously. "Do you know something I don't?" He pretended to feel his chest to check his heartbeat. "Am I dying?"

"We're all dying, Kullen. Some of us faster than others." About to leave, Kate turned back again for a second, her expression far more serious than it had been just a moment ago. "If you tell anyone I said this," she told him in a low, steely voice, "I'll deny it and sue the pants off you for defamation of character, but you're a damn good lawyer, Kullen, and if anyone can go up against Mrs. Dalton's flesh-eating piranhas and win, my money's on you."

The genuinely surprised look on Kullen's face pleased her.

"Because you're quick and you're good. And being my brother doesn't exactly hold you back, either," she added loftily. "Winning against all odds is in our DNA." And there was a major reason for that, one that had been part of their everyday lives. "The old man expected it."

"The old man is probably the one who planted this need to win inside both of us to begin with," Kullen replied.

Their father had been a hard man to please and an even harder man to love. But he'd known that they both loved him.

Kate crossed to the door. "Can I get you anything?" she asked, her hand on the doorknob.

"Yeah, about four hours' sleep." This day was no different from any of the others and it required that he be sharp. Right now, he felt as sharp as a pencil with a broken point. "I didn't really get any last night."

Kate rolled her eyes. "Brag, brag, brag."

He didn't want her getting the wrong idea, not about

Lilli. Or their relationship. "It's not like that. I didn't sleep with her."

Her smile was wicked. Knowing. "In my experience, sleeping rarely comes into it."

"You know what I mean," he said impatiently. Patience was for people who got enough sleep. "There's no physical relationship."

Kate stood there for a long moment, studying him. And then she grinned. "This is more serious than I thought. Mom just may die of happiness. Wow, two in one year. She's hit the jackpot."

Maybe it was his lack of sleep, but he had no idea what his sister was talking about. "Two *what* in one year?"

"You're the sharp lawyer, Kullen. You figure it out," she told him with a pleased laugh just before she walked out and closed the door behind her.

Kullen could have sworn he heard his sister humming a wedding march as she walked away.

It was official, he thought, continuing with his search for the file he needed. The women in his family were certifiably crazy.

Chapter Eleven

For once, Kullen managed to leave work a few minutes early. He took the opportunity to stop by his place and pack a couple of changes of clothing as well as a few other things he thought he might need for his stay at Lilli's.

It felt odd standing on her doorstep with a suitcase in his hand. Odder still when the door opened in response to his knock and it wasn't Lilli—or her son—he found himself looking at, but Anne McCall, her mother.

"Oh. Hello, Kullen. Lilli told me that you'd be over."

The woman, who looked more like Lilli's older sister than her mother, appeared ill at ease in his presence. At first he thought it was because of the suitcase he was carrying, then he realized that her discomfort went deeper than that.

Stepping back to allow him into the living room,

Anne lowered her eyes and seemed to address her words to the rug beneath her feet.

"I want to thank you for what you're doing for Lilli." Then, as if rallying, Lilli's mother forced herself to look up and meet his gaze. She cleared her throat. "About the last time we saw each other…" Anne's voice trailed off for a moment, then returned with a measure of force. "I didn't mean to lie to you…."

So that was what this was all about, Kullen thought. In retrospect he realized that Lilli's mother had to have lied to him, but bearing a grudge seemed pointless, especially after all this time.

"You had your reasons," Kullen told her diplomatically.

Eight years ago, frantic over Lilli having taken off the way she had, he'd felt that if anyone knew where she had gone, it would be her mother. The first personal thing Lilli had ever shared with him was that she and her mother were very close.

But when he sought out Anne McCall, asking after Lilli's whereabouts, her mother had told him that she had no idea where Lilli was. She said that the only thing she *did* know was that Lilli had told her that she wanted to be left alone, and that if he cared anything at all about her, he would just let her go and move on with his life.

Looking at Anne McCall now, that scene between them came back to him in all-too vivid colors. As did the frustration and the ache that had all but torn him apart at the time.

He remembered being on the verge of a deep depression but his spirit, his determination to go on no matter what, mercifully had kicked in. With a great deal of effort—and the need to survive—he had taught himself how to block out that painful section of his life, and all thoughts of Lilli with it. He forced himself to continue because he fervently wanted not to be subjected to his father's lectures if he'd washed out of law school after all the money that had been invested in his education.

Most of all, he didn't want his father to pull his mother into this, angrily blaming her for raising such a "soft" son.

So he'd hardened himself and had somehow gotten through it. At the same time, he'd hardened his heart down to its inner core, allowing no one to get through ever again. Kullen schooled himself not only to be a good lawyer, but to be a good lover as well. He became a lover of women—but never allowed himself to be in love with any of them. Not ever again.

"Yes," Anne said to him after another awkward silence had passed, "I had my reasons and they were to protect my child." She looked at him, a sliver of contrition in her eyes. "But still, you deserved better. You came to me because you cared about Lilli so much. I saw it in your eyes and I still turned you away." Her guilt obviously weighed heavily on her. Anne pressed her lips together, then said, "I'm sorry, Kullen."

He got no satisfaction from her discomfort. It erased nothing, restored nothing. "It's in the past, Mrs. McCall. Please don't worry about it," Kullen counseled.

"Lilli told me what you're doing for her." Her eyes softened as she said, "Thank you."

There was no need to thank him. If something happened to the boy because he'd ignored Lilli's concerns, then it would be on him. The way he saw it, he had no choice. "I'm a lawyer. It's what I do."

Anne shook her head. "I'm talking about the extra mile. Staying here to allay Lilli's fears that that horrible woman was sending someone to steal Jonathan—that's not part of being a lawyer," she said knowingly. "That's part of being a good man." Impulsively, Anne opened the purse she was holding and took out her checkbook. "I don't have much money, but whatever I have, it's yours."

Kullen put his hand over the checkbook, closing it as he shook his head. "We'll work something out later," he promised.

"Yes, we will," Anne replied. Her hand on the door-knob, she paused a moment longer. The glint of tears entered her eyes and she fought to keep them in check. "Your mother raised a good man, Kullen. No wonder she's so proud of you."

Drawn by the voices, Lilli walked into the living room just in time to see her mother finally make it out the door.

But her attention was focused on Kullen. Part of her really hadn't believed that he would return for a second night. But he had, and it brought her a tremendous wave of relief.

"You came back."

He set down his suitcase on the rug beside the sofa. "Did you think I wouldn't?"

"I wouldn't have blamed you if you hadn't," she confessed. She could only guess what he thought about the fears she'd shared with him. To him this had to be a little like holding the hand of a child at night who was afraid of the dark. "In addition I wouldn't have blamed you if you had reconsidered taking on my case and changed your mind about the whole thing."

"Why would I do that?"

She took a breath before answering. "To get revenge for what I did to you."

In addition to the suitcase, he'd brought along his briefcase. He'd set it on the coffee table and was unpacking his laptop, but her words stopped him in his tracks. He looked at Lilli for a long moment.

"Is that what you think of me?" he finally asked, his voice low, devoid of emotion. "That I've been biding my time all these years, waiting to spring some kind of revenge on you in order to soothe my bruised ego?"

When he put it like that, Lilli thought, entertaining the fears she'd had seemed stupid now.

The smile that curved the corners of her mouth was shy and, to him, almost painfully sweet. "No, you're not like that. I don't know why you're not like that because I had it coming to me, but you're not."

He could feel it. Lilli stirred up feelings, memories and a battalion of emotions that would only get in the way of his doing a good job. Emotions that might impede his winning the case for her. They had to be banked down.

"Look, I think this will work out better if we just put the past behind us as if it never happened. Our history is not going to help you retain custody of your son," he said.

She looked at him with a trace of confusion. "What do you mean?"

The history that was important belonged to Erik and

his mother. "I have a private investigator looking into several angles that might prove advantageous to our side, and that's where our focus will be. The only part of your back history that's important is the fact that you didn't sweep this whole episode from your life when you had the chance. You went through with the pregnancy and kept your baby. Another woman—"

Lilli didn't let him finish. She didn't want to even hear him say it out loud.

"There was never any other option," she told him quietly, firmly. "None of what happened at his conception was Jonathan's fault. He was the innocent in all this."

Jonathan picked that moment to burst into the room, going off like a proverbial firecracker. Seeing Kullen, the boy grinned from ear to ear and made a beeline for his new idol.

"Hi, Mr. Kullen, want to play another game of racers with me?" he asked eagerly, his small face shining with hope.

Lilli caught her son before he could successfully launch himself at Kullen. "Jonathan, Mr. Kullen has work to—"

"Sure," Kullen cut in, answering the boy's question. "Can't think of a better way to unwind after a stress-filled day." He put his arm around Jonathan's small, slender shoulders.

Lilli looked at him. Was he just saying that for the boy's sake? "Seriously?" she pressed.

Kullen nodded, still gazing at his small friend. "Seriously."

"All right. Then I'll be in the kitchen, getting dinner ready," Lilli told him, excusing herself.

As she turned to go, Lilli caught her reflection in the living room window. If she grinned any harder, she was fairly certain her face would crack apart from the sheer force.

All things considered, there were far worse ways to go.

The sound of her son's gleeful laughter filled the air, warming her heart.

It was three days later, or rather, three evenings later. Three evenings and she'd already slipped into a routine, looking forward to leaving work to come home to Jonathan and Kullen the way some people looked forward to sipping their favorite drink at night to unwind, or treating themselves to something special as a reward for what they'd endured or accomplished.

This was something special, all right, she thought, watching her son interact with Kullen as the cars they were piloting with their separate controllers raced across the wide flat-screen.

If this was the merit system, then she'd done everything *not* to deserve this cozy scene.

This is what life would have been like if—

If.

But the word *if* didn't apply here. She was a grown woman and grown women didn't believe in fairy tales or happily-ever-after. Life was there, lurking in the wings to show them otherwise, just as it had showed her.

Still…

"Mom, you've got a funny look on your face," Jonathan said, twisting around on the sofa to look up at her.

Lilli flushed, forcing herself to focus. "Sorry, honey," she said, smiling at him. "I was just thinking."

"About what?" the boy asked. They were gathered around the coffee table in the family room. A vote had been taken to allow dinner be an informal affair, nibbled on between serious rounds of the latest video game that Kullen had brought over for Jonathan.

She grabbed at the first thing that occurred to her. "About how nice it was that Mr. Kullen brought over this game for you."

Twisting around to face forward, Jonathan beamed at his idol. "Yeah," he chimed in. "Super-nice. Thanks again, Mr. Kullen."

"You're more than welcome, champ."

Kullen's eyes met hers over the boy's head and held for a long moment. She felt as if he could see into her head. Into her heart. That he knew there was more to her statement than what she'd said to the boy.

Was he doing this because he was kind, or because, perhaps even subconsciously, Kullen was showing her what she'd missed by disappearing eight years ago?

Don't torture yourself with questions you can't answer. Just enjoy this however long it lasts. For once in your life, seize the moment.

Her smile suddenly looked strained, Kullen thought. And he couldn't help wondering what was going on in her head.

He'd told himself more than once not to get pulled into this scenario, not to enjoy these simple pleasures as much as he did, because this whole scene was only temporary. Once he had leverage against Elizabeth Dalton, he could get the widow of the pharmaceutical heir to agree to an out-of-court settlement.

And once it was settled, that would be that.

Lilli would go on with her life and he with his. Separately. He had no illusions that any other scenario was in the offing.

Which was why he wasn't supposed to allow himself to get so involved in the everyday events of this little family.

Easier said than done, he upbraided himself as Jonathan's infectious laughter filled the air. The boy had won again.

Losing, Kullen thought as he congratulated the boy on a race well run, never felt so good.

"You wore him out," Lilli declared walking into the living room later that evening. She'd just finished helping Jonathan get ready for bed. The boy had fallen asleep the minute his head hit the pillow even as he was protesting that he wasn't the least bit sleepy.

Kullen laughed as he glanced up from his laptop. "That works two ways."

Lilli sat down on the edge of what would be his bed in a matter of hours. "You don't look worn out," she commented.

"Practice," he told her, looking back at the screen he'd been reading.

She knew she should go and leave Kullen to his work but somehow, she couldn't seem to make herself get up just yet. She liked watching him. She could remember him looking that intense when they were in law school, studying together for an exam. He was so focused it seemed as if even the roots of his hair were studying.

"Find something to help us?" she asked, trying not to sound as if her whole world depended on his answer.

"Not sure yet," he answered thoughtfully. "So far these are just pieces of the puzzle that Jewel's sending to me."

"Jewel?" A foreign emotion stirred within her. Jealousy? Jewel wasn't his sister's name. A girlfriend, maybe?

And what if she is? The man has a right to a girl-friend, a life. You cut him loose, remember?

Kullen nodded as he continued reading. "The investigator I've got digging into Erik and his mother's past." He looked at Lilli. "Jewel found out that you definitely weren't the first woman Erik sexually assaulted—or the last," he added. "Seems Dalton had the morals of a rutting pig. Kept his mother's most trusted attorney, a Howard Cooper, very busy cutting deals as he cut checks in exchange for the women's silence." Kullen paused. "Did you ever take any money—"

"Not a dime," she declared, angry at the very thought.

"Are you sure?" he pressed, his eyes on hers. He told himself that if she was lying, he'd know. *Yeah, like you figured out what was going on eight years ago, right?*

"Of course I'm sure," Lilli cried. "Don't you think that I'd remember something like that? No one ever offered me money in exchange for my silence or my baby. I would have made him eat it if he had. Why would I lie about that to you?" she asked.

He took an intelligent guess. "Because you're afraid. Because you want to keep your son and you think this might jeopardize that, paint you in a bad light as some- one who could be bought off."

He was just doing his job, she told herself. There was no reason for her to feel as if she was suddenly alone again.

"I'm only going to say this once so listen carefully," she told Kullen. "I never asked for any money, and no lawyer named Cooper or anyone else ever approached me with any money." Her eyes narrowed, fixing him with a glare. "What part of that don't you understand?"

He was honest with her, playing devil's advocate. "The part where all the other victims were given money but not you. Why not?" he asked. He didn't like riddles unless he had the answers, and he didn't in this case. He knew Elizabeth Dalton's lawyers would try to trip him up with this. If Lilli was hiding something from him, he needed to know now. "Why were all these other women paid off and not you?"

"I don't know," she cried, fisting her hands at her sides. Rising to her feet, she began to pace around the room restlessly. She was struggling not to shout, afraid of waking up Jonathan. Because she knew he was only trying to help—even though his question made her an- gry—she searched for an answer.

She gave him the only one she could come up with. "Maybe because I never went to him, and all the other women did," she guessed. "I wrote him a note only after Jonathan was born and that took a lot for me to do. I didn't tell Erik where I was, didn't ask him for anything. I never wanted to see him again, *ever.* I had a friend who was a flight attendant mail the note from another state.

I did it for Jonathan so I could tell him that his father knew about him if he asked me someday."

"And you never gave Erik an address, or told him how to get in touch with you?"

"No!" she retorted. "Don't you understand? I didn't want to see him, didn't want anything from him," she said fiercely, then struggled to control her voice. She realized that she was all but shouting at Kullen. Getting control over herself, she nodded at the laptop. "How many half brothers and sisters does my son have?"

He looked at the screen although he didn't have to. What he'd read was pretty conclusive. "From what I can tell, none."

"None?" she echoed. How was that possible? The law of averages didn't bear that out. "But you said that he'd forced himself on other women. It sounded like a lot of other women—"

"According to what Jewel found, the ones who did get pregnant terminated their pregnancies the minute they were paid off."

She stared at him. "All of them?"

He nodded, scrolling through Jewel's notes. "Looks like all of them," he confirmed. He glanced up at her. "This is probably why Elizabeth Dalton is so obsessed with getting custody of your son. Unless I missed something or Jewel hasn't found it yet, from the looks of it, Jonathan is her only living grandchild. Her only family, now that Erik's dead."

Lilli sank back down on the sofa as the weight of what he was telling her penetrated. She really was in for the fight of her life.

Kullen took out his cell phone and pressed a number

in his directory. A moment later, he heard the phone on the other end ringing.

"Hi, it's Kullen. Got a minute? I just had a chance to go over the preliminary report you emailed. Great work, by the way. Did you get anything on Mrs. Dalton yet?"

Lilli watched his face and surmised the negative answer. She suppressed a sigh.

"Okay, keep me posted and call me the minute you find anything," Kullen requested, terminating the call.

As he put his phone away, he slanted a glance toward Lilli. She had an odd expression on her face he couldn't read.

Chapter Twelve

Kullen waited, expecting her to ask a question. When she didn't, he decided that Lilli needed a little prodding. The look on her face had aroused his curiosity—as well as, he had to silently admit, other things.

"What?"

She supposed that constantly internalizing her concern wasn't the healthiest way. Remaining silent left her thinking the worst.

"Your investigator didn't find any skeletons in Mrs. Dalton's closet, did she?" she asked.

He saw the disappointment in her eyes. And the deep concern. In general, he wasn't a glass-half-full or half-empty kind of guy. The glass was what it was.

But in this case, once again he felt that Lilli needed some hope. "No, not yet, but give her a little more time."

Lilli wanted so much to believe that it was going to be

all right. She looked up into his eyes, silently pleading. "Tell me it's not hopeless."

He knew that Elizabeth Dalton was a force to be reckoned with, but he also believed that the justice system did prevail for the most part. "It's not hopeless."

Lilli nodded, but it was clear that she was vacillating between feeling hopeful and consumed with worry. "Because if it is," she continued, "then I'd better start packing."

"Packing?"

Again she nodded. "I'm not letting Elizabeth Dalton get her hands on Jonathan. She'll wind up turning my son into another Erik, I know she will."

"I doubt that. He's your son. He has your values. Even at this age, you can see that he's not a weakling, not easily bent."

"I really hope you're right," she told him with heartfelt sincerity. "But I'm not taking any chances. I was willing to let Mrs. Dalton see Jonathan, let her be part of his life like any normal grandmother. But that wasn't enough for her." She vividly remembered the moment when the woman seemed to turn on her. "She told me that she wouldn't take a backseat to anyone. And that I wasn't fit to raise a Dalton. I told her that Jonathan wasn't a Dalton, he was a McCall. She laughed at me and said that just proved her point, that I was more of a lightweight than she thought."

There was anger in her eyes, Kullen noted, as she continued. Damn, but she was magnificent, he couldn't help thinking.

"Any doubts I had that keeping Jonathan would ultimately result in depriving him of the finer things in life died right then and there. I'd rather have him poor, but well-adjusted and happy than a rich and self-centered bastard like…" She couldn't bring herself to finish the sentence. "Well, you know…."

"His father?" Kullen supplied.

He hadn't expected to see the very real flash of anger that crossed her face. "Erik wasn't his father," she insisted. "He doesn't deserve that title. He was just a sperm donor under the worst possible conditions."

Every time he thought of what she'd gone through at that sick bastard's hands, he wanted to find some way to make it all up to her, to make the incident disappear from her memory. He wanted to hold her, but he remembered how she initially froze when he hugged her. He had no doubt that he would have to start at square one, and he didn't want to do anything to jeopardize their professional relationship. The best thing he could do for her was to be her lawyer.

"Leave your suitcases where they are," he instructed. "As I told you, the courts tend to side with the mother in these kinds of cases."

Lilli was not nearly as confident as he was. Before coming to him she'd done her research on Elizabeth Dalton. Some organizations had all but canonized the woman.

"Unless the person seeking custody is a well-known philanthropist who has half the city fawning over her and thinking she's some kind of saint. Do you know how much money she's donated to Blair Memorial Hospital alone? How do I win against someone like that? The family court judge will be falling all over himself or herself to give Mrs. Dalton what she wants."

"Why don't you let me worry about that?" he suggested. "We might come up with some pretty persuasive arguments yet. As Yogi Berra said, 'It ain't over till it's over.'" He smiled at the ironically worded statement. "A lot of truth in that."

God, but she hoped he and Yogi were right. "Sorry, I'm predisposed to worrying." She lifted her shoulders in a helpless gesture, then let them drop. "I think it's congenital."

"You know what you need?" he asked. "You need to get out, to have a little fun. To forget about all this for a few hours."

She doubted if she could put this out of her mind for even five minutes. Retaining custody was all she thought about, waking *and* sleeping.

"After we win."

He was thinking about before the court date. Otherwise, she would be so tightly wound that by the time they won, she'd be a basket case, unable to enjoy her son. "Unless Jewel can come up with something very soon, winning might take us a while. You've got to make an effort to wind down. I need you relaxed and in control when we walk into the courtroom."

"I can be in control," she told him confidently. As for the other, she doubted if that was possible, given her present state of mind. "But relaxed…" Her voice trailed off. There was a skeptical look on her face.

"I've got a wedding I need to attend this Saturday," he began.

Her eyes met his. "All right."

Why was he telling her this? she asked silently. Was he saying that he would not be here with her and

Jonathan this weekend? Or was there something else coming? She missed the optimistic, happy person she'd once been, the person who Erik had killed that night he'd forced himself on her.

"Come with me," Kullen urged. The moment the words were out of his mouth, he knew it was the right thing to do. He wanted her with him and what better, safer setting than a wedding, where there would be scores of other people around.

"What?"

"The invitation is for me and a guest," Kullen explained, liking the idea more and more. "You can be my guest."

The thought of being with him on what would ordinarily be seen as a date warmed her. Tempted her. But even as she toyed with the thought, she knew she had to remember what was important here. She shook her head, turning him down. "I don't want to leave Jonathan."

"You don't have to," he assured her. "He can be half a guest," he teased.

She'd forgotten how endearing Kullen could be. "Really?" She felt amusement tugging at the corners of her mouth. "Is that how your invitation reads? Kullen Manetti and one and a half guests?"

"Not quite," he conceded. "But it can be arranged. Jonathan is small, he won't take up much room." It was an outdoor wedding. Another chair could be pulled up. "You've got to learn not to fight me on everything," he told Lilli. He gave her a quick summary of the situation. "One of Kate's best friends, Nikki, is getting married. Kate and her other best friend, Jewel, are the maids of honor."

"Jewel," Lilli repeated, alert. "Is she the same one you just—"

"Yes," he confirmed. "I've known the bride—and Jewel—ever since Kate started bringing them over to the house when she was in third grade."

What was it like to have friendships that went back that far? After she had learned she was pregnant, she had distanced herself from everyone who had ever meant anything to her. Lilli supposed she couldn't blame it all on Erik. She was the one who was responsible for that.

"You don't have to explain anything to me," she told Kullen. "I understand."

"I'm not explaining," he corrected. "I'm just giving you some background." He looked at her pointedly. "I think it'll do you good to come, Lilli. To unwind a little. Being uptight isn't going to help you any at the trial," he repeated.

What would Jonathan do all that time? "I can't just drag Jonathan to a wedding."

"No dragging involved," Kullen promised. "And there'll be other kids there around his age. My mother and her cronies will be there, too. I guarantee they'll be fighting each other for the right to watch Jonathan for us."

Us. He'd said *us,* not *you.* Was that just a slip of the tongue, or did he see himself that way? As part of a couple?

You know the answer to that. You had your chance and you let it slip through your fingers.

She cleared her throat and asked, "Why would they need to watch him?"

He did his best to keep a straight face as he answered, "So you won't worry about him being alone at the table when we dance."

"Dance?" she echoed. And then, despite her apprehension, her lips curved in a real smile.

"Yeah. Dance," he repeated. "It's what people do to music when they can't sing to it. You must have heard of it. I hear it's catching on all over the country."

She laughed, tickled despite the oppressive gravity that was never far from her mind. "Yes, I think I remember hearing about it somewhere."

"Good, then I won't have to draw any diagrams for you." The idea of dancing with her warmed him as he thought about it now.

"Don't be so sure about that," Lilli warned. "The only one I've danced with in a very long time is Jonathan. When he was a baby," she added, then explained. "It would soothe him and he'd go right to sleep." She smiled fondly, remembering. "If I dance with you, I might put you to sleep."

That was the last thing that dancing with her would do. "I sincerely doubt that," he told her. "Although," he proposed, "if you're game, we can put your theory to the test."

Her immediate reaction was to draw back. It was ingrained in her. Another reason to hate Erik and to keep her son from falling into his mother's clutches. "No, that's all right—"

"Afraid?" he challenged loftily, playing a hunch.

The single-word question had the desired effect. He saw Lilli's chin lift, saw the stubborn look that entered her eyes. The Lilli he remembered had been soft-spoken and meek. The one who had walked into his office to ask for his help had more spirit than her younger counterpart. He was fairly certain that being a mother, being solely responsible for a child, had created this newer, braver Lilli 2.0.

He'd seen that transformation occur in his own mother when his father had died. Suddenly widowed, Theresa Manetti had one of two choices. Either crumble, or meet life head-on. His mother had chosen the latter and so, obviously, had Lilli.

Without answering him, Lilli walked over to the radio and turned it on, switching to the CD that was already loaded. When the disc clicked into place, she pressed another button, selecting a song.

As a popular singer's timeless voice filled the air, she marched back to Kullen and silently presented herself to him.

He took her into his arms.

Just as he did, a little voice inside her head whispered, *Idiot, now you've gone and done it. Mayday! Mayday!*

But it was too late to back away. Unless she wanted to look like a fool.

What could it really hurt? she reasoned. It was only one dance.

So she let Kullen take her hand into his and place it against his chest. Let him slip his other hand around her waist, and let him draw her to him, her body fitting against his as if it had finally come home.

She was an adult, Lilli argued. She could do this without any consequences. After all, she wasn't an inexperienced schoolgirl, barely out of her teens, not anymore....

So why did it feel as if she was?

Why was she trembling? She realized, too, the increase in temperature. By at least ten degrees, if not more. That was the reason why she felt so incredibly hot. Either that, or she had just come down with an instant case of malaria.

This was a mistake, Kullen thought.

A big one.

Up until now, he'd been doing all right—as long as none of his body parts came in contact with hers. The moment they made contact, he could *feel* it. Feel the latent desire taking up every available nook and cranny within him.

The desire to hold her, to caress her, to make love to her the way she had never had love made to her, all but overwhelmed him. He knew that the popular concept revolved around the word *with,* but in this case, it would definitely be *to.* Lilli deserved to be made love *to,* to be held and revered and treated with dignity, respect and the utmost tender affection.

He ached to do all three.

While he would never, ever violate her boundaries, he was having one hell of a time holding himself in check. Moreover, it was growing exponentially harder and harder with each passing second.

"Maybe this isn't such a good idea," he told her, his voice strained as every fiber in his being was at war with itself.

"Why?" she whispered, afraid of what she was feeling. And even more afraid *not* to be feeling it.

She felt dizzy and giddy and excited all at the same time.

"Because," he told her honestly. "Holding you like this makes me remember how much I wanted you."

"Wanted?" she repeated. There was a ribbon of sorrow in her voice, as if she regretted what might have been but no longer was. Regretted a loss of what she had never been allowed to experience. "Does that mean you don't anymore?"

The question was barely audible. She'd raised her face to look into his eyes as she asked the question. Kullen felt her breath gliding along his neck. Felt his gut tighten.

He could barely breathe. She literally took his breath away.

Kullen hardly remembered the precise moment his control shattered. One minute, he was dancing with her to an old, familiar melody as a vocalist sang about the love he'd lost. The next, he'd stopped moving and was kissing her as if his very life depended on it.

The moment his lips touched hers, memories came racing back. Swept away, Kullen scooped her up in his arms, raising her off the floor in his zeal as he lost himself in the feel and the taste of her.

It had been eight long years, with too many women in between to remember. Not a single one of them had come within a mile of generating what he felt right at this moment.

There was a reason for that.

None of those women had ever been anything more than poor placeholders for the only woman who had ever mattered to him. The only one who had ever taken his heart prisoner.

He kissed her again.

And again.

And again.

And she kissed him back. Not hesitantly, not tentatively, the way he'd expected, but with passionate ardor.

Desire exploded in his veins.

Nothing else mattered but having her. And yet, he knew he couldn't. He couldn't sweep her away, couldn't assume she was feeling what he felt.

He could only ask. And silently pray he was right. If he wasn't…he couldn't even bring himself to contemplate the possibility.

So with the greatest of efforts, Kullen drew himself back from her, his heart pounding like hail on a tin roof in a bad winter storm.

"Lilli—" he began, not knowing how to ask, how even to form the next word.

"Shh."

Breathing hard, Lilli placed her finger to his lips, silencing him. This wasn't the time for talking, for reasoning. For doubts. She wanted to feel alive, not frightened, not worried.

He made her feel alive. She wanted him to go on doing that.

But as she pressed her mouth to his, Killen pulled back again one last time, even as he wondered where in heaven's name he found the strength.

"Lilli, are you sure?" he asked her, then repeated

more forcefully, "Are you sure?" all the while praying that her answer was yes.

Sure?

No, she wasn't sure. She wasn't sure of anything. But she did know that with him, with Kullen, she was safe. He made her feel safe. And he wouldn't hurt her. She had no idea where this confidence about his motives came from or how she knew, but she did.

And knowing allowed her to gather up all the feelings, the emotions that Erik had shattered, and let them go. Kullen helped her feel whole again. The man who would save her son.

She wanted to feel cherished, not used. Feel as if she mattered, feel that he wanted *her,* not just a body with a pulse. Most of all, she wanted him to block out the dark memory that Erik had branded on her mind.

On her toes, her arms wound around his neck, Lilli whispered into his ear, "Show me what it *can* be like."

And just like that, she became his undoing.

He felt as if he had a mandate, a responsibility, and he intended to do right by it. Do right by her. Lifting Lilli in his arms, he kissed her again just before he began walking toward the staircase.

What he had been charged to do, what every fiber in his body was poised to do, needed privacy. Needed to be done behind closed doors so that there would be no sudden interruptions, breaking the mood. No interruptions stealing the moment.

He intended to make love *to* her and then *with* her, the way they both ached to have happen.

And he needed to begin right now, before he burned away to a crisp.

Chapter Thirteen

With her cheek resting against his shoulder, Lilli could feel every breath he took. Her adrenaline ramped up another notch as Kullen came to the landing. He didn't put her down.

"First door on your left," she whispered, holding on to him tightly.

The door to her room stood open, but not for long. Crossing the threshold, still holding her in his arms, Kullen pushed against the door with his back.

The soft click told him that the door was closed, but not locked. And seven-year-olds had a habit of having nightmares—he could still remember the ones he'd had. The last thing he wanted was for Jonathan to come bursting in, half-asleep and needing comfort, only to see something he shouldn't witness.

Lowering Lilli until her feet touched the floor, Kullen reached behind him and turned the lock so that it caught and held. When Lilli looked at him, one eyebrow raised, he told her, "So that Jonathan doesn't get traumatized."

Warmth instantly flared inside her. Even as she got caught up in the moment, he had the presence of mind to think about her son. They didn't make men like Kullen anymore, she thought.

But even as she got lost in him, Lilli could feel a distant sadness threatening to seep in. She'd had her chance to marry him and turned her back on it. Her disappearance might have been for the best of reasons, but she had still rejected his proposal. Rejected her chance at happiness.

The memory made her want to seize this moment before it was gone, too. Before the phone rang or something else happened to take him away from her.

Or make him come to his senses.

With thoughts like that to spur her on, Lilli wrapped her arms around his neck, leaned into him and kissed him with all the intensity and longing that ravaged every single space inside of her.

Damn, but she was making this difficult, Kullen thought. When she kissed him like that, his very blood caught on fire. Restraint took almost superhuman strength.

But he had to restrain himself.

He wanted to do this slowly, to make love as if there was nothing else to do for the next eight hours. He wanted to touch her, to caress her, to love Lilli with his whole being.

He wanted to worship her.

Kullen had no idea if there had been any other men

in her life after she'd run off. In the time they'd been together, she'd made no mention of anyone but that didn't mean that there hadn't been someone special between then and now. He had no way of knowing if a boyfriend had taken the care that he should have in making love with her, but whether the answer was yes or no, Kullen knew that he fully intended to do that now.

There was no way—even fleetingly—that he wanted Lilli to think of that animal who had assaulted her.

Kissing her slowly, deepening each kiss a little more than the one that had come before, Kullen could feel his own knees threaten to buckle. Forcing himself to focus, he began to tug the hem of her blouse out of the waistband of her pencil skirt.

When he began to push the shirt's buttons through their holes one at a time, he heard Lilli's sharp intake of breath. Was that evidence of excitement he heard, or fear?

Not taking any chances, he drew his lips away from the hollow of her throat and told her in a low, husky voice, "You can stop me at any time. If anything I'm doing makes you uncomfortable, tell me. I'll sto—"

Kullen didn't get a chance to finish. Lilli had sealed her mouth urgently to his. Succeeding in making him utterly crazy—and loving it.

What came afterward happened in a kind of haze. The chain of events became a jumble in his head.

He must have finished undressing her because Lilli was perfectly nude beneath his palms as he passed them over her. His heart hitched in his throat as he tried to absorb the sensations created in his belly.

His hands skimmed along her soft, firm skin. Somewhere along the line, amid the bursts of red-hot passion erupting through his body, Lilli must have returned the compliment and undressed him as well because there he was, separated from his clothing, his skin burning for the feel of hers.

Pushing her gently down onto the snow-white comforter, he began to cover her supple body with a shower of light, teasing and, he concluded from her reaction, incredibly arousing kisses.

By pleasuring her, he was driving himself crazy. Each time she reacted, the echo of passion grew even louder within him, demanding things he was trying to hold off doing until he felt that she was ready. But he was determined to go only as quickly as she wanted.

Although her yearning had roots that went back eight years, Lilli admitted that she was afraid of what was ahead. Afraid that making love with Kullen would propel her back to that dark place.

But this was nothing like that other time.

What Kullen was doing was in a different league. He had lit fires within her and he treated her as if she were made out of spun sugar. She could feel the urgency within him, but she could also feel that he held back. Even so, he touched her so lightly with his hands and his lips that she could feel needs vibrating within her, almost pleading for release.

He was an artist and she was his canvas. A hungry canvas ready to absorb every stroke, every nuance. He made her feel things. Good things. Things that made her blood rush and her head spin.

She wanted him.

Wanted him to seal his body to hers.

Wanted to be one with him.

But when she raised her hips to his in a silent invitation, rather than fill her the way she expected him to, Lilli suddenly felt his breath travel lower on her skin. And lower again.

Her stomach muscles quivered as anticipation roared through her limbs.

He went lower still.

Suddenly, explosions ripped through her veins, carrying her off to where the sky was filled with a plethora of incredible, heated colors. She grasped sections of the comforter beneath her with both hands as sweet agony filled her.

His mouth was hot, his tongue quick, gentle and wildly arousing. She had to bite down hard on her lower lip to keep from screaming out his name as a climax rocked her very core. One sensation flowered into the next like a Fourth of July fireworks display.

For a second, there seemed to be no end.

Exhausted, she let a low sigh escape as the sensations finally receded. She would have hugged the world if she'd been able.

Lilli realized that her eyes were shut, as if that somehow enhanced the experience. Feeling a little foolish, she opened them and saw that Kullen had drawn himself back up to her level again, his eyes on hers.

Before she could tell him how wondrous the whole experience was, he had covered her mouth with his own. And then he was directly over her. Rather than completing the action of becoming one with her, he drew back and looked at her. There was concern in his eyes.

"Is it all right?"

Because he had asked, it was. His kindness, his concern effectively erased all her fears, dispelled any remnants of the memory that had haunted her for so terribly long.

She whispered yes, and felt him entering gently. The act completed, they were temporarily fused into one. Everything throbbed within her. She anticipated more. Was eager for more.

And then, there was more.

Kullen began to move his hips, igniting her even as she mirrored his movements, his tempo.

They raced each other up the side of the mountain, then experienced the last seconds of this transient paradise together.

At the last second, the gratifying euphoria seized him. Kullen hugged her hard. So hard that he was afraid he had bruised her ribs if not broken them outright. For a split second, he'd had trouble controlling the lightning-fast surge she had generated in him.

"Sorry," he murmured, releasing her.

The word echoed like a hoary insult, hanging just above her heart, hurting more than physical daggers.

"Sorry?" she repeated, feeling her heart constricting. Why was he doing this to her? "Sorry you did this?"

Where had she gotten that idea from? Kullen wondered, staring at her. Erik Dalton had not only stolen her innocence, the slime bucket had shattered her confidence as well.

"No," Kullen corrected patiently, "sorry if I squeezed you too hard."

"Oh," she acknowledged quietly. When he raised himself up on his elbow to look at her, there was an expression of satisfaction on her lips that seemed to penetrate down to the very bone.

Just as it did within him, he thought.

Slipping his arm beneath Lilli, he pulled her to him, affection building inside him. It occurred to him that he would have been perfectly happy to remain like this with her indefinitely.

His career would eventually go to hell, he reasoned whimsically, but his soul would be happy. It seemed like a good trade-off to him right now. But she was being too quiet. "I didn't hurt you, did I?" he asked.

"No," she replied softly, "you didn't hurt me." But there was something she had to know. Lilli searched for courage to form the words. "You weren't…" Her courage flagged, her voice faded.

Instantly alert, knowing he had only a tiny window of time to clear up any misunderstanding, he pressed her to finish. "I wasn't what?"

"Disappointed, were you?" she finally managed to get out. Did that sound as egotistical to him as it did to her? But she wasn't looking to get her ego stroked, she just had to know if she'd failed him.

"Disappointed?" he repeated incredulously. Very slowly, he ran his knuckles lightly along her jawline. He saw a spark of desire flare in her eyes. "I've been wanting to do that for eight years. And it was everything I thought it would be—and more."

She appreciated what he was trying to do, but she knew how inexperienced she was. Until just now, her only sexual encounter had been that one awful time when she'd been assaulted.

"You don't have to lie," she told him, lowering her eyes.

"I know I don't. And I'm not," he added in case she still had misgivings. Shifting, he moved so that he could look into her eyes. "Lilli, please, don't let what happened to you eight years ago scar you forever," he entreated.

Anger mounted inside him, all but choking him. Had Erik Dalton not been dead, Kullen would have been sorely tempted to call the lowlife out and beat him within an inch of his worthless life. Or maybe even to go further than that.

There was such a thing as justifiable homicide, he thought darkly, and if anyone ever deserved to be sent to their maker in a pine box, it was Erik Dalton. The fact that the man had died as a result of an accident didn't provide the right kind of satisfaction.

"You should have told me," he said, lightly brushing her hair away from her face. "Eight years ago, when it happened, you should have told me about it."

But Lilli shook her head. "I didn't really get to know you until afterward." She pressed her lips together, not wanting the old feelings of guilt and regret to find her. "Let's not talk about it now."

"Okay." He didn't want to mar this moment with bad memories. "No talking. What'll we do then?" he asked, pretending to ponder the dilemma. "Oh, wait, I think I know."

The next moment, he lightly trailed his lips and tongue along the hollow of her throat, resurrecting desires she'd thought had all but burnt themselves out for the duration of the night.

Instead, they were back in full force.

Within a moment, she found herself breathing hard all over again, as if she'd run a marathon. Or was anticipating running one.

"You're kidding," she managed to get out. "You can do this again so soon?"

"I take vitamins," Kullen cracked in between kisses that turned her into a proverbial puddle. And then he stopped, growing serious. "Unless you don't want to—"

"I want to," she assured him. "I'm experience challenged, not mentally challenged."

"What you might lack in experience," he told her, "you more than make up for with enthusiasm."

To prove it, he sealed his mouth to hers. And felt her smile beneath his lips. It was all he needed to reignite the not quite dormant fires within him.

"So that's a yes?" he asked the next morning the moment she opened her eyes.

Morning was casting a subdued light into the room. He'd been watching her sleep for a while now and feeling incredibly peaceful. Whatever happened from here on in, he would always have the memory of last night to sustain him.

Still reveling in the afterglow of last night, Lilli blinked and tried to pull her thoughts together. She drew a blank on what he was talking about.

Oh, God, she suddenly realized, she had to look awful. He wasn't supposed to see her like this, looking like a used rag doll whose stuffings had been yanked out. For a second, she had an impulse to throw the covers over her head, but that was not an option. Kullen had pinned the covers down under his torso when he'd rolled over in her direction.

As her brain slowly engaged, she noted that he was leaning on one elbow, looking at her. How long had that been going on? Was he having second thoughts now, wondering what act of charity had possessed him last night to make love with her?

She cleared her throat, trying not to sound like a frog that had just leaped out of the pond. "What's a yes?"

"Nikki's wedding." She still watched him blankly. "You'll come with me?" he prodded. "You and Jonathan," he amended, before she could tell him again that she didn't feel right about leaving the boy home, even if her mother was there to watch him.

It took Lilli a second to connect the dots. And then a little longer to think everything through. She'd thought he was just making small talk about taking her to the wedding.

"You still want to take me?" she asked, surprised.

"Sure. Why not? We can't let all that dancing we did last night go to waste," he reminded her, his face unreadable.

"As I recall, we didn't do that much dancing," she replied.

He gave up the ruse and grinned broadly, then pressed a kiss to her shoulder.

Waves of desire shimmied all through her, making her want him with a fierceness that was completely foreign to her. She liked the feeling and savored it, knowing that she was on borrowed time. One way or another, this would be over with all too soon.

"Yeah," he said, his eyes seducing her, "I guess we didn't. Want to not dance again?"

He was wicked. And delicious. He made her feel so incredibly wonderful it didn't seem quite possible. And yet, it was.

"Don't you have to go to work?" she asked him.

"Eventually," he conceded. "But man does not live by work alone. What I have in mind is taking care of matters of the soul."

She couldn't keep the smile back. It took over her whole face. "Is that what you call it now?"

"Yup."

The next second, he'd rolled over, partially pinning her to the mattress with his body. But even as he did so, he left her a space where she could wiggle free if she so chose.

But she didn't.

There were no more words between them for a while. They had other ways of communicating. And only a limited amount of time.

Chapter Fourteen

It utterly amazed Lilli how easy it was to fall into a routine with Kullen. To look forward to her evenings to a degree that she never had before. Having Kullen around made her feel safe, secure.

And it excited her at the same time.

Feeling this way caused Lilli to reevaluate her life, to reevaluate her conceptions about herself. For years she'd been convinced that she would never be able to be at ease with a man, to have intimacy. She'd assumed that what had happened to her that awful night would forever wedge its way into any relationship she had if it began to turn physical.

But she was wrong.

Or maybe this was such an exception because it involved the right man. And Kullen was right on *so* many different levels.

Maybe this would work out for them, for her, after all.

Don't get carried away, she cautioned herself. *Don't start hoping and losing your heart. You walked out on Kullen once, it's going to be a long haul before he really trusts you with his feelings again. If ever.*

And besides, Kullen was in a different place in his life back when they were in law school together. Now his needs were different, and his tastes had evolved.

For all she knew, she might be good for a dalliance but not as the woman he wanted to spend the rest of his life with. And who was to say that she was actually ready for that kind of commitment? She was finally taking tiny baby steps forward. She could finally allow a man—*this* man—to touch her. To make love with her. But baby steps didn't mean she was suddenly ready to undertake a marathon and make a wild dash for the finish line.

Lilli put down her mascara wand and sighed. There was no doubt about it. She'd never felt so summarily confused before in her life.

Confused, and yet looking forward to hearing the doorbell ring each night around six. Looking forward to seeing Kullen standing on her doorstep, that same funny, lopsided smile on his lips that had won her heart the first time in law school.

Time had passed. They'd both grown up, and yet one simple smile and she was catapulted into the past. One simple smile and all over again he was that endearing kid she once knew.

Lilli picked up the mascara wand and continued getting ready. Kullen was coming by to take her and her son to a wedding and she didn't want to keep him waiting.

God, how wonderfully normal that sounded. How

long had it been since she'd even felt remotely normal instead of going through the motions? Looking over her shoulder, afraid that Erik had tracked her down, wanting a second encounter?

Feeling normal, that was all Kullen's doing, she thought, smiling at the reflection of the woman in the mirror. And for however long it lasted, she was determined to enjoy it. It would help her fill a little of the emptiness that lay in wait for her later.

"Mom?" Jonathan called, obviously looking for her.

"I'm in my room, Jonathan," she answered, raising her voice so that he could hear her. "Just putting the finishing touches on my makeup." Retiring the wand, she leaned over the sink to reapply light touches of pearl-blue eye shadow.

Jonathan came in wearing a small tuxedo that her mother had picked out for him. The boy was momentarily sidetracked as he looked at her. "You don't need all that makeup stuff, Mom," he protested. "You're pretty already."

Lilli laughed. "And you have a wonderful dating future in front of you," she prophesied. "You'll have to beat the girls off with a stick."

Jonathan looked perplexed. "But you said never to hit a girl," he reminded her. "Is it okay if I use a stick to do it?"

Amused, she ruffled Jonathan's wheat-colored hair a little. "No, you're right, it's never okay to hit a girl. That was just an expression I used. I'm sorry, I didn't mean to confuse you."

His quick smile was bright and forgiving. "That's

okay, Mom." Just then, the doorbell rang. His eyes suddenly shone with enthusiasm. "I'll get it!" he announced.

He was quick, but she was still quicker. She caught his arm before he could make good on his announcement. "*We'll* get it," she corrected.

With a sigh, Jonathan headed toward the front of the house, matching what he called his mother's poky pace. But it was obvious that he wanted to run to open the door. "But it's Mr. Kullen," Jonathan protested.

"Most likely," she agreed. "But it's better to be safe than sorry." She didn't want to scare him, to make him see things in the shadows, but on the other hand, if anything ever happened to him, she would never forgive herself.

Jonathan pursed his lips and looked up at her thoughtfully just as they came to the bottom landing. The smile faded. "You think it's the man?"

She looked at him sharply. "What man?"

"The man in the tree," Jonathan answered her without missing a beat.

Almost at the front door, she stopped and once again caught hold of Jonathan's arm. She turned him around to face her.

"*What* man in the tree?" she asked. Although she was fairly certain that Jonathan was just remembering a nightmare, she could feel her adrenaline kick in. Just in case he wasn't talking about a bad dream, she needed to find out as much as she could.

"The one I saw with a big ol' camera," Jonathan answered matter-of-factly. "I think he was taking pictures from the branch he was on."

"Taking pictures?" she repeated. This had to be a dream—right? The doorbell rang again, but her attention was completely focused on what Jonathan was telling her. "When did you see him?"

"Last night. And the night before that." He paused to count in his head. "And maybe two times before that. Maybe the pictures weren't coming out," he said, guessing why the mysterious tree dweller kept coming back.

Fear gripped her throat. "You *saw* him four different times?"

He nodded his head up and down. "Uh-huh. Mom, you're squishing my arm," he protested, trying to pull it free.

She released him and dropped her hand. "Sorry, baby, I'm just trying to think. You sure you didn't dream this?" she pressed, hoping against hope that he would take back what he'd just told her. He had a very vivid imagination.

Jonathan lifted his shoulders in the exaggerated shrug that all small children emulate when they have no answers. After a second, he let them drop again.

"I dunno. Maybe." The doorbell rang a third time. "Aren't you gonna let him in?" Jonathan asked, seeming upset that his new best friend was being kept outside.

"Yes, I'm going to let him in—after I make sure it's him," she stressed.

Pausing to look through the door's peephole, Lilli verified that Kullen stood on the other side and not some tree-climbing stranger whom she'd been blissfully unaware of a scant five minutes ago.

Taking a step back, she opened the door to admit Kullen.

As he entered, Kullen was about to comment that he'd begun sprouting roots on the doorstep, but the words evaporated from his tongue. Instead, he whistled low in appreciation. His eyes swept over her, taking in every subtle detail. She wore a soft gray-blue cocktail dress that was several inches shy of her knees. The dress was intimately familiar with every single curve she possessed.

It made him want to skip the wedding and just take her back upstairs to her bedroom. Lucky for both of them that Jonathan was there to keep him grounded. Kate and his mother would simply kill him if he missed Nikki's wedding.

Lilli flashed him an apologetic smile. "Sorry, I didn't mean to keep you waiting."

"Not a problem," he assured her. "The view was definitely worth waiting for." Belatedly, he remembered to flash a greeting at the boy. "Hi, champ. You ready to go?" he asked.

"Ready," Jonathan announced, all but hopping up and down.

Kullen's gaze shifted over to Lilli. "Something wrong?" he asked, then added, "You look a little preoccupied."

Jonathan beat his mother to an answer. "Mom's worried about the man in the tree."

The easy smile on Kullen's lips instantly vanished. His whole body went on red alert. "What man in the tree?" The question was directed toward Lilli.

"Jonathan said he saw someone in the tree last night taking pictures."

There was a tree situated on the side of the property. Though not directly against the house, its position afforded a view of both Jonathan's bedroom and Lilli's, too. It wasn't close enough to allow someone to clamber into the house. So why was someone climbing it?

"When?" Kullen asked.

"Last night," the boy piped up. "And maybe three other times. But I can't remember for sure."

Kullen didn't want to alarm the boy. He kept his voice light, friendly. "And you're sure that you saw someone in it?"

"Uh-huh." His head bobbed up and down. "Taking pictures."

"Could it have been a dream?" Kullen suggested, mentally crossing his fingers.

"I already asked him that," Lilli told him. "But it seems pretty unlikely that he'd have the same dream three different times, much less four."

"Not as unlikely as you'd think," Kullen contradicted. "I once had the same dream every night for a month."

What he didn't add was that the dreams had been about her, about finding her after she'd run off and talking her into coming back. Waking up each morning to reality had all but destroyed him and had come perilously close to sending him into a deep, dark depression.

"Maybe," Jonathan conceded slowly, answering Kullen's question.

Leading the way to his car, Kullen lowered his voice so that the boy couldn't readily hear him. "Maybe he overheard us talking about being worried that he might be kidnapped and this is the result," he suggested to Lilli.

She nodded. "Maybe." At least she could fervently hope so.

After all, she silently argued, what was the point of climbing into the tree and just watching the boy without doing anything? It *had* to be a dream. Otherwise, it didn't make any sense.

She got into the passenger side while Jonathan scrambled into the backseat. He dutifully buckled up. Lilli listened for the telltale click of the metal sliding into the slot.

To her surprise, Kullen didn't get in behind the steering wheel. Instead, he went back to the house and then started to move slowly around the perimeter.

She stuck her head out of the car. "What are you doing?"

"Just checking out a hunch." Kullen tossed the words over his shoulder as he disappeared around the side of the house. Lilli continued to watch the furthermost corner, waiting for him to reappear.

It felt as if she was staring for a long time.

When he emerged again, he was walking quickly.

"Everything's okay," he told Lilli, getting into the car. Slamming the door shut, he reached for his seat belt. "No footprints," he added.

The look of relief on her face made the little white lie he'd just told her worth it. While there were no actual footprints around the tree, there was a reason for that. The tree in question was deciduous. Consequently, it had dropped more than half its leaves, all of which made a rich carpet for any intruder, tree-climbing or otherwise, to use without leaving any footprints.

Hence, whether or not the boy had seen someone in the tree was inconclusive. But for now, Kullen thought it best not to make Lilli worry, perhaps needlessly. Allaying her fears was his job.

So was making sure that nothing happened to her or the boy, he thought. Bottom line was that, his playboy title notwithstanding, he always took his work seriously.

Turning the key in the ignition, he started the car up, announced, "Here we go," and they roared out of the driveway, much to Jonathan's delight.

He kept up a steady stream of conversation with the boy and Lilli, and for a while thoughts about tree-climbing intruders and the threat they posed were pushed aside.

Kullen made a mental note to ask Jewel to install a surveillance camera at Lilli's house while she was away at work. If someone turned up at night, spying on Jonathan, he wanted footage of it—to use in court if need be. He had no doubts that if Jonathan hadn't dreamed up this mysterious person, whoever he'd seen was on Elizabeth Dalton's payroll.

A sigh of contentment escaped from her lips.

"That has a nice sound to it," Kullen commented, slipping his hand over hers. He was sitting beside her at the outdoor reception.

"It all feels so wonderfully normal," Lilli told him as she watched Jonathan play with a couple of children who had come to the ceremony with their parents. Bored at the reception, the children played a game of hide and seek between the tables.

Kullen followed her line of vision toward her son. He'd briefed his mother and her two best friends about the situation—and the possible intruder in the tree—so he was now assured that, not counting his own, at least three pairs of eyes were on the boy at any given moment.

"That's because it is," Kullen told her. "*Very* normal."

"I'd forgotten what normal felt like," she confided. He could hear her smile in her voice. "What anything but standing guard, vigilant, felt like." She turned her face toward his, leaning her cheek against the palm of her hand. "It feels good. Thank you."

"You're welcome," he murmured. He felt guilt pinching the perimeters of his conscience over the deception he purposely conducted, even if it was for her own good. He saw no reason to make her more anxious until he had some definite proof.

"If you really want to thank me…" he began.

The glass of champagne she'd had wound its way through her, making her feel incredibly light-headed. And incredibly grateful. But there was a danger in that. A danger in allowing her thoughts to take flight. More than likely, disappointment lurked in the shadows.

"Yes?" she prodded.

Instead of answering right away, he rose from the table. On his feet, he put his hand out to her. "You'll dance with me."

She pretended to sigh. "Well, it's a dirty job, but I

guess I do owe you." Placing her hand in his, she pushed her chair back and rose to her feet.

He led her to the makeshift dance floor that Lucas and his father, an ex-Navy SEAL who had flown in for the wedding, had set up the night before. There were several couples already there. Kullen staked out a small area for them.

"You don't owe me anything," he told her seriously. Taking her into his arms, he began to dance. It was a slow dance and he hoped it would go on forever.

"Oh, but I do," she protested, trying to fill her brain with rhetoric and not think about how well they fit together. How much she wished that they could go on fitting together until the world ran out of time. "And I always pay my debts."

He nodded, letting the light perfume she wore fill his head. It turned out to be a tactical mistake since the scent filled the rest of him, nudging desire awake in his belly.

"Good to know," he murmured against her hair.

Lilli tried not to shiver, tried not to behave like some adolescent who was hopelessly enamored for the very first time in her life. But that was exactly what she was. She'd never really been in love, other than falling for Kullen—twice. Once when she'd finally managed to block out the effects and repercussions of what Dalton had done to her—just before she found out she was pregnant. And now, here she was again, loving the same man.

Except that this time she knew she was living in a fool's paradise. That happily-ever-after was an unattainable state because she'd treated Kullen so badly the first time around.

And she really couldn't blame him. In his place, she would probably react the same way. Happy about getting together again but nonetheless waiting for the other shoe to drop. Waiting for history to repeat itself. Anything she might say in the way of protest or in her own defense would have the feel of "the lady doth protest too much."

You can't expect the dog that bit you to live up to his word that he won't bite you again, she thought ruefully.

And, in this case, she was the dog.

They danced by the head table, where Nikki Connors, now Nikki Connors-Wingate, sat with her brand-new husband, Lucas.

Lilli couldn't remember when she'd seen a bride look so happy. She found herself envying Nikki.

"She's a beautiful bride," Lilli commented to Kullen.

Kullen laughed softly. "Haven't you heard? All brides are beautiful," he informed her. "It's an unwritten law somewhere."

She looked at him in surprise. And then she smiled in appreciation. "I had no idea you were such a sentimentalist, Kullen."

He watched her for a long moment. "There are a lot of things about me that you don't know," he told her gently.

The softly spoken words flowed along her skin, warming her. Making her yearn. With all her heart, Lilli wished that she would be given the opportunity to uncover all those secrets he carried around with him. Slowly, over a lifetime together.

But she knew better than that. Some things, no matter how much she wanted them, just weren't destined to happen.

Chapter Fifteen

As it turned out, Kullen and Lilli were among the last guests to leave the wedding reception.

He had it bad. It warmed him simply to watch her. Lilli was having such a good time socializing with his sister and her friends, he didn't have the heart to cut it short. But eventually, his sister caught the bouquet, the bride and groom left for their honeymoon, the band packed away their instruments and it was time for even those who were lingering to go. He and Lilli collected a sleepy-eyed Jonathan from Theresa, said their good-byes to Maizie and the father of the groom, who had been extremely attentive to Maizie throughout the evening, and left.

One mile into the trip back home, Jonathan fell asleep in the backseat.

"Looks like we finally found a way to tire Jonathan

out," Lilli commented, turning around in her seat and looking at her son as Kullen pulled into her driveway.

Getting out of the car, Lilli opened the rear door and undid her son's seat belt. She was about to pick the boy up when Kullen gently nudged her out of the way.

"I've got him," he told her, scooping the boy up into his arms. He nodded toward the house. "You just unlock the front door."

"Okay." Tired, she flashed him a grateful smile and hurried up the driveway.

Lilli disarmed the security system so that the three of them could go inside without setting off any alarms. Turning, she watched Kullen come up the walk, Jonathan safely tucked against him.

Her heart fluttered, moved, as she stood there, committing the scene to memory. It would be something for her to remember when life got to be a little too much for her.

This was the way it was supposed to be, in a perfect world.

Jonathan continued sleeping even as Kullen carried him upstairs and laid him down on the bed. Lilli decided to forgo changing the boy out of his clothes and into his pajamas. Sleep was more important than wrinkles in a miniature tuxedo, she reasoned.

Stepping back from her son, she felt Kullen taking her hand. They silently slipped out of Jonathan's room together, taking care to leave the night-light on and ease the door shut.

Once in the hall, she turned to him. "Thank you for talking me into going. I had a wonderful time. It was so great to forget about everything for a while," she said with feeling. "To just enjoy myself, watching Jonathan play with kids his own age." She smiled up into Kullen's eyes. "Dancing with you."

"Is that so?" he deadpanned. "I don't remember dancing with Jonathan."

"Idiot," she laughed, taking a swat at his shoulder. "I meant *my* dancing with you."

He surprised her by suddenly twirling her around and pressing her up against the wall, his body invading her space.

"The evening's not over," he reminded her. Bracketing her face by placing his hands against the wall on either side of her, he then leaned in for a sensuous, soul-draining kiss that left her all but gasping for air. And relishing the fact that he sounded a bit breathless as well.

"Love evenings that aren't over," she managed to whisper, her head spinning.

It would always be this way, she thought. For whatever time she was with him, Kullen would make her feel this way. He would make her pulse race and her head swirl about, make excitement roar inside her body.

"Glad to hear it," he murmured just as his mouth came down on hers.

And he was right, she thought, as he swept her into his arms. The evening was gloriously far from over.

Morning arrived all too soon.

The only saving grace was that this was Sunday morning. Sunday meant she didn't have to go in to work because the shop was closed. Sunday meant being able to curl up a little longer beside this man whose presence she didn't remotely take for granted, not for a moment. Each time she and Kullen made love, she was even more acutely aware of how tentative this all really was.

And how special.

Stretching languidly in bed like a waking feline, she was about to get up and see about making breakfast for the three of them when Kullen abruptly pulled her back into bed. Surprised, she felt her back hit the mattress, and the next moment his body tantalizingly covered hers. He was careful to distribute his weight across his elbows. The light contact created a need for more within her. She looked up at him quizzically,

"Where are you going?" Kullen asked, teasingly skimming his fingers along her body. "It's early."

"I was going to get dressed and go down to the kitchen to make breakfast for all of us." He was still strumming along her skin, driving her crazy. Rendering rational thought impossible. "You know, food."

"I'm more interested in food for the soul than for my belly," he murmured, lightly kissing the side of her face, working his way down to her neck.

He was weaving his magic again, casting his spell over her. Making her want more. She knew she should behave responsibly and insist on getting up. But she didn't hear Jonathan stirring, and who knew how much longer she would be allowed to remain a visitor in this paradise Kullen had created for her?

She was all too aware that this could all change. Tonight, tomorrow, a week from now, she had no idea how much longer she would be allowed to enjoy being with Kullen like this. There was absolutely no reason for her to suppose that once the case was over—and God willing Kullen would secure sole custody for her—he would still be coming around.

It was more likely that he wouldn't. That didn't mean that he was taking advantage of her now—if anything, she was taking advantage of him. What it did mean was that once the case was over, Kullen would be moving on to another case. A case that would require all his attention.

And there would be none left over for her.

Even thinking about it created a sharp pain in her gut.

So she put breakfast and the rest of her life on hold and lost herself in the fiery world that Kullen could create for her with just the touch of his hand, the feel of his lips on hers.

"Food for the soul it is," she declared softly, entwining her arms around his neck and pulling him even closer to her than he already was.

They made love with the excitement of two people on the threshold of a brand new world, not like two people who had just ventured into this same territory a few short hours ago.

It was the same.

It was different.

All she knew was that it was wonderful and she would miss it desperately when she went back to being the only one sleeping in her queen-size bed.

Spent, with the delicious feel of euphoria still holding her in its warm embrace, Lilli thought she heard music playing.

Drawing herself up on her elbow, she looked at Kullen. "Do you hear something?"

That was when he suddenly jackknifed into a sitting position and reached across her body to get to her nightstand. As his body touched hers, a tantalizing shiver danced up her spine.

Was she ever going to get enough of him?

She knew the answer to that. It was no.

"It's my phone," Kullen told her as he moved back to his side of the bed, the cell in his hand. He flipped it open and put it to his ear. "Hello?"

Her body tingled all over again from the short, intense contact and she took a breath to steady her erratic pulse.

"Who's calling you at this hour on a Sunday?" she heard herself asking.

But even now he was holding up his hand for her to hang on to her questions until he finished talking—or listening—to the person on the other end of the call.

The ensuing silence made Lilli uneasy.

Who was on the other end and what were they saying? Instinct—or maybe it was paranoia—told her it had to do with her. With Jonathan and her. She felt certain she was right. Kullen's back was rigid.

Sitting up, she tried to peer around his side to catch a glimpse of his face.

Before she could, she heard him say, "You sure about that, Jewel?"

Okay, so it was Jewel calling him. She assumed that the woman had something to report about the case, although it amazed her that the private investigator was working this early. Jewel had stayed at Nikki and Lucas's wedding reception nearly as long as she and Kullen had. What could she have found out between last night and this morning?

But then again, maybe Jewel had been working an angle all along and it had just panned out now. Kullen had told her that Jewel was one of the best at what she did and didn't stop until she got what she was after.

"Okay, thanks. Great work," Kullen said with enthusiasm. "I'll pick them up later today if it's all right with you. All right. Noon it is. I owe you. Beyond the fee," he insisted, obviously answering a disclaimer Jewel must have made.

Lilli could hardly contain herself, waiting for Kullen to finish his call. When he did, she immediately pounced on him.

"What was that all about?"

Twisting around, he grinned at her. "Information," he said evasively.

"I *gathered* that," Lilli countered, trying to keep her impatience under wraps. "What *kind* of information?" she pressed.

For the second time this morning, Kullen caught her off guard and pulled her to him. He kissed her long and hard before finally answering.

They were officially in the home stretch, and he had no idea how things would play out once the case was over. He knew what his hopes were, but he'd had those same hopes before and it had gotten him a boatload of heartache.

"Okay," he said, moving her back a couple inches. "I've got some good news and some bad news."

She needed good news desperately, but ending on

a down note, especially right now, might just be more than she could handle, so she opted to hear the bad first, hoping that the good news would more than balance it out.

"Okay," she said, bracing herself, "what's the bad news?"

"Elizabeth Dalton wants another meeting with me." He'd known that Friday evening, but there had been no way he was going to spoil the wedding for Lilli, by telling her. She would have been second-guessing why the woman wanted to see him until the face-to-face meeting finally came about.

The meeting was set for Monday and now, thanks to his hunch and to Jewel's diligent investigation, he was going to be far from empty-handed when he met with Mrs. Dalton.

"Why's that bad?" She had her own sinking suspicions, but she wanted to hear it from him.

"Because Mrs. Dalton is certain that she has information that will guarantee her getting custody of Jonathan."

Lilli's breath backed up in her chest. So much so that it took effort to get her words out. "And what's the good news?"

He didn't want to go into details just yet. "I think we've got something that'll trump that."

God, she hoped so. But from everything she'd read about Elizabeth Dalton, she never went into a fight unless she was armed to the teeth. What if what they had turned out to be a shield made out of tissue paper? "What does she have?"

He thought of saying that it was best for now if she

didn't know, but he had a feeling she would wheedle it out of him. Kullen decided to spare them both this process of bobbing and weaving like two prizefighters.

"Pictures," he told her simply.

She cocked her head, confused. "Pictures?"

"Of us," he added.

Was she missing something? "Why's that a problem? You're my lawyer." She pointed out.

He looked at her pointedly. "Pictures of us," he repeated, adding the proper emphasis on the last word.

Us.

And then it dawned on her. He had to be referring to pictures that were a huge, embarrassing invasion of their most private moments together. Her hands flew to her mouth. She couldn't be right. He had to be talking about something else. Oh, please let him be talking about something else.

"Oh, my God, are you saying—"

He saw she understood and nodded slowly. "Yes, I am. Apparently the man in the tree that Jonathan told us he saw really wasn't a dream. What he saw was one of Mrs. Dalton's flunkies, taking pictures of us—not Jonathan—with a telephoto lens."

Lilli wanted to cry. She felt numb—and violated at the same time.

The rest wasn't hard to guess. "And she intends to have her lawyers say that I'm an unfit mother because I'm having an affair with my lawyer."

Kullen nodded. "That is undoubtedly her game plan," he agreed.

Lilli leaped out of bed in a heartbeat. She was so agitated, she didn't seem to realize—or care—that she didn't have on a stitch of clothing. She had to get Jonathan and herself out of here.

Who knew how much time she had left before someone from social services was knocking on her door? She wouldn't put it past Mrs. Dalton to pull the rug out from under her in the cruelest fashion imaginable. And losing her child to the massive tangle of red tape that social services embodied would definitely be it.

When Kullen caught her by the wrist a second time, she tugged, this time with a great deal of urgency. She could have saved herself the trouble. His grip was incredibly strong. He wasn't about to let her go running off.

"Let me go, Kullen," she pleaded. "I've got to pack our things. Who knows how much time Jonathan and I have before the roof caves in."

"You're getting carried away," he told her in a steady, low-key voice.

"No, I'm not."

Didn't he understand? Or was it that he didn't really care? He was doing this as a favor to her. If it didn't pan out, oh, well, he'd tried. Was *that* how he felt about it? She didn't want to think about that. There wasn't time enough for that, or hurt feelings. She had to save her baby.

"I won't let that woman get her hands on Jonathan," she cried fiercely. "I'll kill her first."

He wondered if, at bottom, she was capable of that. When pushed to the wall, a lot of people reacted atypically compared to their normal behavior. Lilli might be no different, although he would have liked to believe that she was.

"I wouldn't go advertising that if I were you."

"Why are you so calm?" she demanded, frustrated. He should be helping her, not holding her back.

Unless—

"Wait," she cried, staring at him. "Does how calm you're being have anything to do with that call you just took from Jewel?"

He smiled at her. "It has everything to do with that call I just took from Jewel," he told her. And then, maddeningly, he gave her a platitude. "Have a little faith, Lilli." He kissed her forehead as if to brand her with the philosophy. "Now, if you really want to make breakfast, I suggest you put something on because if you keep standing like that in front of me, I really am going to wind up having something else to eat for breakfast," he told her with a wicked grin.

She was too nervous to dally with him again, no matter how tempting the idea might be. Her heart wouldn't be in it.

Because her heart was severely worried.

"I'll get dressed," she told him, extracting her wrist from his grip.

As she hurried off to the closet, she felt just the tiniest bit better. Kullen wouldn't be teasing her like this if she was about to lose custody of Jonathan.

At least, she fervently prayed that he wouldn't.

For her own sanity, she pushed the thought from her mind. Pushed everything from her mind and concentrated on putting one foot in front of the other, praying that eventually, it would lead her from here to there—and *there* would be someplace where she actually *wanted* to be. With her son.

* * *

"Why can't you tell me exactly what this magic 'weapon' you have is," Lilli asked between her clenched teeth. She and Kullen stood waiting for the door to Elizabeth Dalton's mansion to open in response to the doorbell he had just rung.

It was Monday morning and although she'd sent Jonathan off to school with her mother, there was no way she could pretend that it was business as usual. For one thing, she hadn't gone in to work, asking one of the sales clerks to open today. For another, she had argued her way into going with Kullen to his meeting with the woman who had the power to summarily ruin her life.

Or rather, more specifically, the power to turn her and her son into fugitives.

She'd meant what she'd told Kullen on Sunday. If her back was to the wall with no other choice open to her, she was willing to kill Elizabeth Dalton before she would allow the woman to touch her son.

Since it wasn't part of her inherent nature to kill insects, much less a person no matter how odious, the next best thing for her was to vanish. And that meant turning her son and herself into fugitives.

It also meant, she suddenly realized, never seeing Kullen again.

The very thought of that all but ripped her heart out of her chest.

Just as Kullen had said that his had been ripped out when he'd discovered that she'd disappeared, leaving behind the engagement ring he'd given her.

She slanted a glance at Kullen. She wanted to tell him she was sorry. She wanted to tell him that she loved him even though this might be the last time they were together.

She wanted to say so many things, but now was not the time. So she kept her peace and pressed her lips together, praying that there would *be* another time for them when she could say all that.

The door opened just then and the same dour-faced man, Terrence, greeted them with a curt nod. His small, deep-set eyes focused on Kullen.

"Mrs. Dalton's been expecting you," Terrence said to him. And then, squinting, the tiny brown marbles shifted toward Lilli. "But not you."

Chapter Sixteen

Before Lilli could open her mouth to voice her protest, Kullen spoke up on her behalf.

"Ms. McCall has a right to be at this meeting, especially since it involves the question of her son's custody," Kullen informed the tall, unsmiling man. Although mildly friendly and conversational, there was no room for argument with his tone.

And, after a moment of what appeared to be somewhat annoyed reflection, Terrence obviously decided that it was in his best interest not to argue. With another curt nod of his head, the dour man bit off, "Follow me," turned on his heel and walked into the exquisitely decorated, oversize mansion that had all the warmth of a mausoleum.

As before, Elizabeth Dalton sat waiting for Kullen in the library. There was a manila envelope on the coffee table before her.

Regal, poised and extremely confident, the woman's smile faded when she saw that this time Kullen had brought his client with him.

The breath Mrs. Dalton dramatically exhaled testified to her displeasure. "When I said I wanted to see you, Mr. Manetti, I meant you in the singular form, not the plural."

Without waiting for an invitation, Kullen sat down on the sofa beside the woman.

After a beat, Lilli sank down on the love seat that faced the sofa. She couldn't bring herself to sit any closer than that to Elizabeth Dalton.

"Since everything we say here is going to affect Ms. McCall, I see no reason she should be kept away from this meeting," he told Mrs. Dalton.

Elizabeth slanted a look toward the woman she regarded as just a shade above dirt and smirked.

"Very well, I was attempting to spare her some embarrassment, but upon reflection, she's undoubtedly accustomed to being embarrassed on a regular basis." Dismissing Lilli's presence as not worth her attention, Elizabeth turned back to Kullen and what really mattered here. "I asked you here as a courtesy. I want you to drop all opposition to my custody suit, or my lawyers will be forced to enter these photographs into evidence to show the court just how unfit your client is to raise my grandson."

So saying, Elizabeth withdrew several black-and-white eight-by-ten photographs from the envelope and carefully dealt them one by one across the surface of the coffee table as if she were distributing giant playing cards. The small, smug smile on her lips grew deeper when she heard Lilli's sudden sharp intake of breath.

Elizabeth sat back on the sofa, admiring the photographs she'd paid a private investigator a fortune to take.

"As you can see, these are all quite damning." She raised eyes the color of blueberries to Kullen's face. "Although I must say, Mr. Manetti, you have a spectacularly athletic body under those impeccably tailored suits. I never would have guessed if I hadn't seen these photographs myself."

"How dare you!" Lilli cried. "It's not bad enough that your son ripped apart my life, now you want to take your turn at it, too?"

Elizabeth's eyes narrowed to reptilian slits as she regarded Lilli. "I will dare anything to get what I want, and I want my grandson."

"You can't—" Lilli stopped abruptly and looked at Kullen, who had just grabbed her arm. "What?" she demanded, fighting the urge to pull the woman's carefully styled blond hair out by its roots.

"It's okay, Lilli," he assured her in a voice that was almost maddeningly calm and controlled. "No one's going to see these photographs."

"Not if you relinquish your claim to Jonathan's custody," Elizabeth underscored confidently.

"I don't need to 'claim' custody, I *have* custody," Lilli declared angrily. "He's my son."

Rather than try to calm Lilli down, Kullen focused his attention on the woman creating these emotional tidal waves. Opening his jacket, he took an envelope of his own from his inside pocket.

He took what he needed out of the envelope. "I'll see your compromising photographs and raise you these," he told the older woman in a cheerful voice, lining up his photographs directly beneath hers.

"What are these?" Elizabeth demanded impatiently as her anger flared. "What are you talking about?"

"I'm talking about your late, although far from great, career, Mrs. Dalton. Or would you prefer I call you by your stage name, Hard-hearted Hannah? If I'm not mistaken, you got that name from an old song. But then, these photographs are from a long time ago, too. Another lifetime, I dare say.

"Still, if you look closely, there is no mistaking the true identity of the athletic young woman in these photographs." He looked up at Mrs. Dalton. "I had no idea that a human body could actually bend to that extent. You possessed an exceptional talent."

Elizabeth Dalton had gone pale, even as her eyes widened. "Where did you get those photographs?" she demanded hoarsely.

He was in no hurry to tell her everything in short sound bites. He let her twist a little, as he was certain she had done to Lilli.

"Well, technically," he began slowly, carefully realigning the photographs, "they weren't photographs to begin with. These are stills taken from a compromising video. I apologize for the quality, but I had to work with what I had." The note of regret in his voice mocked her. "I wonder what the board members at Dalton Pharmaceuticals would say if they saw these. Or maybe I'll just burn copies of the original video for them. One copy for each of them. What do you think?"

"You wouldn't dare." There was a dangerous note in the woman's voice, but she no longer had any idea who she was dealing with. She had assumed that a playboy like Kullen would go for the easy fix, talking his client into going along with what was expedient.

Kullen didn't even blink. "Oh, I think we both know that I would. And it would be such a shame, too, to destroy your reputation after you've spent half a lifetime carefully crafting it and bolstering it with all those generous donations to charities. But I assure you it can be done, Mrs. Dalton. The public, as I'm sure you already know, loves to fawn and elevate almost as much as it likes to revile and tear down. Guess which category you'll fall into?" he asked with a complacent smile.

Before she answered, he continued. "My guess is that a story like this about a person of your high standing will go viral in a heartbeat and continue with themes and variations ad nauseum for quite some time. I can hear the morning-show hosts vying for exclusive interviews with you and anyone who's had any contact with you since you were six."

Impotent rage—because she knew when she'd been outmaneuvered—brought the color back into Elizabeth's cheeks. "What do you want?" she ground out.

"Nothing beyond your capacity to give," Kullen informed her.

Leaning over the coffee table, she opened a finely carved ebony box and extracted a checkbook and pen. She glared at Kullen, pen poised.

"How much?"

"It's not a matter of money, Mrs. Dalton," he told her, confident that she already knew that. Kullen nodded toward the photographs he'd laid out. "I can make this all go away if you give up the custody battle."

Instead of agreeing, Mrs. Dalton defended her actions, even though it had been more than three decades since she'd had to resort to anything remotely resembling an explanation, much less a defense.

"I'm not a monster, Mr. Manetti. I was trying to do right by the boy, the way I apparently hadn't by his father."

Kullen remained unmoved, but he did counter her claim. "Leaving him with a mother who loves him more than her own life *is* doing right by the boy."

"You can still see him," Lilli put in. Both Elizabeth and Kullen looked at her in obvious surprise. It wasn't hard to guess that her silence had made them both temporarily forget that she was even in the room. "On holidays and his birthday, you're welcome to come over for a visit."

"What if I wanted him to come here?" Elizabeth challenged stubbornly.

Though Lilli was soft-spoken, she was no longer easily intimidated or led around. She knew what she wanted and she wasn't anyone's pushover anymore.

"Maybe sometime in the future," she allowed, "but for the time being, Jonathan and I will have to respectfully decline," Lilli replied. "The choice to accept my invitation or not is yours."

Disgruntled, unwilling to capitulate to someone so young, Elizabeth turned her attention back to the lawyer. When everything else was stripped away, at bottom she was a survivor and she intended to survive this as well.

"All right," she bit off, "I'll have my lawyers withdraw

the claim." Her eyes narrowed. "I want the tape you have and those photographs." She began gathering them up even as she spoke.

Kullen pushed the rest of the photographs across the table toward her.

"And the original tape?" It wasn't a question so much as a demand. She put her hand out, waiting.

Kullen made no move to produce anything. The tape was housed in a safe place, one he didn't intend to disclose to the woman. "For now my firm is going to hang on to the original tape."

Elizabeth's dark eyes narrowed into small, angry slits. "Until when?"

"Until Jonathan's eighteenth birthday," Lilli told her before Kullen could answer. "Mark your calendar. You can come to his birthday party and I will turn over the original tape to you. But not until then."

Elizabeth didn't say anything immediately. Instead, she sat there, frustrated that she had no options open to her. She wasn't accustomed to losing control.

"You're a gutsy little bitch, aren't you?" she finally said.

Lilli took no offense. If she wasn't mistaken, there was a faint note of admiration in the older woman's tone. It was the first sign of respect Lilli had ever received from her.

Lilli pulled no punches. "Much like you were, I'm told, when you married a much older Donavan Dalton."

Elizabeth pursed her lips as she glared at her. And then, slowly, the glare receded. She turned toward Kullen. Her reputation was everything to her. Far more important than a grandson she'd only glimpsed twice.

When she finally spoke, her voice was begrudging, but resigned. "You have a deal, Mr. Manetti."

After the initial profusion of thank-you's from Lilli, a strange silence between them slipped into the car as Kullen drove her home.

He reasoned that she was overwhelmed and drained. She had been under a huge emotional strain these last few weeks. He assumed that, from one standpoint, it was difficult to wrap her head around the fact that she was finally free to enjoy her son without fear getting in her way, causing her to keep looking over her shoulder.

Still, as the silence stretched out, he found it to be more than a little disconcerting. Granted, Lilli wasn't the type to babble, but he'd never known her to be speechless, either. Especially at a time like this.

Was something wrong?

Taking the exit ramp off the freeway, he decided to plunge in. "Well, it's finally over. Now at least you can stop worrying about having to run off into the night, and go back to moving forward with your life."

He'd even brought the paperwork with him for Mrs. Dalton to sign, rescinding all claims to Jonathan's custody. He'd gone into the office late Sunday evening to get the proper papers drawn up. He intended to file them as soon as possible, closing the book on this case, and giving Lilli her life back, perhaps for the first time in years.

Now it was a done deal. Lilli was no longer his client. He couldn't help wondering, did that leave the door open, or shut?

She'd been staring at her hands, unseeing, for the last fifteen minutes, fighting a mounting, overwhelming sorrow.

There was no longer an excuse for him to be with her every night, no reason for him to stop by. Would it all end right here? Was this just an interlude for him, nothing more? Would she fall victim to the proverbial "out of sight, out of mind?"

The knot in her stomach told her she would. Her heart refused to believe it.

She had to know, had to ask. "I guess I won't be seeing you anymore then."

Her words hit him with the force of a pitched rock. Just like that? She could walk away just like that? Again?

His grip tightened on the steering wheel as he flew through a yellow light on the verge of turning red. "Are you asking me or telling me?"

She wasn't going to cry, she told herself, fiercely struggling not to. She didn't want him to remember her crying.

"Is there a difference?" Lilli asked in a flat whisper.

Maybe he wasn't reading her right, he thought. Oh, God, he hoped he wasn't.

"Well, yes," he told her patiently. "If you're *telling* me, that means you're severing ties. If you're *asking* me, that means that maybe you don't want those ties severed just yet." He glanced in her direction as he eased to a stop just shy of the intersection.

She didn't know what he wanted to hear. She refused to be the clinging woman he kept around just because he thought she couldn't stand on her own. But at the same time, if that was the only way she could keep him in her life, the temptation was huge—

No, she silently insisted, it was wrong. She couldn't make him stay. That would destroy anything they'd had together, however briefly it had existed.

Again she took the direct route. "What do you want me to say?"

He didn't want to put words into her mouth, didn't want to hear her reading off invisible cue cards he'd forced on her. Hearing her parrot the words wouldn't mean anything to him. He wanted her to tell him the truth. Even if it ripped him apart again.

"What's in your heart, Lilli?" he asked. "I want you to tell me what *you* want to say."

Still staring at her clenched hands, she loosened them, prayed and then looked up. "No."

He waited for more. There wasn't any. He tried to make sense out of what she'd just told him. "You won't tell me what's in your heart?"

"No," she told him hoarsely. "The word *no,* that's what's in my heart."

The single, isolated word made no sense to Kullen as it hung in the air before him. "No?"

She nodded her head. If she clasped her hands any tighter in her lap, she was certain her fingers would snap off. She tried hard to loosen them, but somehow, she couldn't. Not yet.

"That's right. No. No, I don't want this to be over and,

no, I don't want this to mean that I won't be seeing you anymore."

Without realizing it, they'd reached her neighborhood and he'd just driven onto her cul de sac. Kullen pulled into her driveway. After turning off the engine, he remained in the car, afraid that a change of venue would change the words around somehow.

"Keep going," he urged.

This was hard for her. But then, maybe if it were easy, it wouldn't have all these emotions involved.

"I was wrong last time." Her eyes met his. "Wrong to leave you like that. But I really thought I was sparing you—and me. Mostly me, I guess." This was hard, she thought. Harder than she'd imagined. But she refused to allow herself to look away. "I didn't want to see the look of loathing in your eyes."

"Loathing?" he repeated incredulously. Now she *really* wasn't making any sense. "Why the hell would I loathe you?"

She pressed her lips together a moment to keep them from trembling. After a moment, she continued. "Because I was pregnant."

"Well, it's not as if you actively went out and campaigned to get that way." Didn't she know him at all, he wondered. Didn't she understand how much she meant to him? How much he loved her, both then and now? "You're missing the salient point here, Lilli. You suffered through a horrific trauma. You were raped and didn't let it defeat you. You came out of it with your head held high, raising a pretty cool kid. That's pretty damn admirable in my book."

Unbuckling his seat belt, Kullen shifted behind the

wheel. He looked into her face and lightly skimmed the back of his knuckles along her cheek. He could feel himself aching for her.

"Of course, if you would have let me, I would have helped you carry that burden so you wouldn't feel as if you were alone."

She knew that now and mourned the years that they'd lost with one another. "I'm sorry about that."

What was done was done, there was no changing the past. Only the future. "It's behind us."

She had to learn how to forgive herself. To forgive herself and focus on the positive side. And there were so many positive things, she realized. Starting with him.

"I really don't know how to thank you—or your mother for giving your name to my mother." Without Kullen fighting for her, for Jonathan, she knew that things could have gone abysmally wrong.

He pretended to consider her words. "If you really mean that, I have a way for you to kill two birds with one stone."

Bemused, she cocked her head as she looked at him and waited. "I'm listening."

"Well, if you marry me," he told her as simply as if he was talking about his plans for the weekend, "you'll make me—and my mother—extremely happy."

Had he just said what she thought he had? She refused to believe that she could get this lucky, not just once but twice. Still, it did sound as if he'd just asked her to be his wife.

"If I marry you," she repeated, stunned.

He watched her eyes for a sign of what her answer would be. "Those were the words."

She shook her head, trying to clear it. She stared at him in sheer wonder—and joy. "You still want to marry me?"

"I never stopped wanting to marry you," he said simply.

Her heart went into double time. "You're serious."

"I could take an oath in blood if you like. Messy, but definitely to the point." He watched as tears slid down her cheeks. Oh, damn, did this mean no? He didn't know if he could handle her turning him down again.

"Why are you crying?" he asked uneasily, taking out a handkerchief and giving it to her.

She wiped her eyes and did her best to look presentable—she didn't want him changing his mind. "Women cry when they're happy."

He was still rather uncertain about this turn of events. "So those are happy tears?"

Handing him back his handkerchief, she felt a smile rising up, taking over not just her lips but her whole countenance. "Yes."

One last tear rolled down her cheek and he touched the tip of his finger to it. He examined what he could.

"They don't look any different than the other kind," he commented. "Are you sure you're happy?"

"Oh, yes," she assured him with feeling. "I'm very sure."

It was as if his whole system just breathed a huge sigh of relief. "Then does that mean that we're finally going to get married?"

She was grinning now. Grinning and happy and giddy beyond belief. "Yes."

Shifting again, Kullen dug into his pocket. Finding

what he was searching for, he took her hand and slipped the ring on.

Her mouth dropped open as she stared at the tiny sparkler. And recognized it. "Is that the same ring?" she asked hoarsely.

"Yes."

She raised her head to look at him. He was far more precious to her than any diamond ring. "You kept it all this time? Why?"

The shrug was quick, dismissive. All his initial silent pep talks to himself about remaining strictly professional with Lilli had been just that: talk.

"Because I guess, at bottom, I'm still an optimist. When you came back into my life, I started carrying the ring in my pocket again—hoping that if and when I gave it to you, you'd keep it this time."

She had to be the luckiest woman on earth, Lilli thought. "I will definitely keep it this time," she told him, holding her hand up so that the infiltrating moonlight could see it, too. "I promise."

"A promise is no good until it's sealed with a kiss," he told her solemnly.

She was more than happy to oblige. "One sealed promise coming up," she told him.

And Lilli was as good as her word.

Epilogue

Lilli had always loved Christmas when she was a little girl, but it had been a long time since she'd felt that pure, innocent joy surging through her about the holiday— the way she felt it now.

And that was Kullen's doing, she thought, circling the ten-foot tree in her living room. She examined it from all angles for the umpteenth time. *He* had made it special for her.

Made it magical.

And busy. Infinitely busy. Tomorrow was Christmas day, and she was opening her house up not just to Kullen's family and friends, but to Elizabeth Dalton, Jonathan's *other* grandmother, as well.

Their house, Lilli silently corrected herself as she adjusted a section of garland that was dipping a little lower than the rest of the string. Opening up *their* house.

She would have to get used to thinking in the plural, not the singular.

Lilli glanced down at the three-week-old wedding band that sparkled and shone on her finger. There were a lot of adjustments to be made. And she was looking forward to making all of them. Lilli smiled to herself. After shouldering her way through life on her own for too long, she was overjoyed at being part of a couple. Part of a family.

The word warmed her.

Family.

And it wasn't referring to just the tight threesome that she, Kullen and Jonathan comprised. No, in this case, the word included Kullen's family as well as her mother.

And Jonathan's other grandmother, she added, thinking of Elizabeth.

She was making good on her promise, inviting her to spend the holiday with Jonathan and the rest of them.

She was nervous about that. Her fingertips turned cold just at the thought of being in the same room with the woman again so soon. But Kullen had promised to be there for her every step of the way, and as long as he was she could face anything, even Elizabeth Dalton.

Surprised, Lilli sucked in her breath as Kullen silently came in and encircled her waist from behind. The scent of his cologne filled her head as he leaned his face in against her cheek.

"I take it Jonathan's finally asleep," she guessed.

"Took three stories, but yes, Jonathan's finally asleep." Still holding her, Kullen pressed a kiss to the side of her neck. She allowed a small, contented sigh to break free. "You ever going to stop fussing around that tree?" he teased.

She turned around in the circle of his arms, several strands of tinsel in her fingertips, tinsel she was presently moving from a branch that had more than enough to one that didn't. "I just want everything to be perfect tomorrow."

Kullen shook his head, amused. She'd been working on that tree for hours, even after he and Jonathan had helped decorate it. "You'll be here—that'll make it perfect."

Lilli relaxed a little, smiling up at him. "I can't remember. Were you always this good with words?"

"Always," he answered with no hesitation.

She laughed. "And modest. Incredibly modest."

"Yes, there's that, too." He took the strands from her and tossed them haphazardly at the tree. They landed in a glob on a branch. She began to reach for them, but he drew her back. "Leave it. It looks more natural that way," he said, kissing the other side of her neck. That was when he noticed a stack of neatly wrapped boxes beneath the tree. They stood out because there was nothing else under it yet. "What's that?" he asked, nodding at the stack.

She glanced over her shoulder to verify what he was referring to. "Your presents."

That wasn't what they'd agreed on. "I thought we were going to let Santa deliver them later, in case Jonathan woke up and came down here before morning."

He'd made her so incredibly happy, she couldn't resist putting a few of the things she'd gotten him under the tree now. "Santa just made a quick pit stop," she explained with a vague shrug. "He'll be back later with the rest of the loot."

"Oh, well, Santa's elves haven't wrapped your gifts yet," he told her. He'd never been good at things like that. For the most part, he thought of himself as gift-wrap-challenged.

"Oh, I wouldn't say that." Lilli's eyes skimmed over him significantly. "The biggest gift of all is standing right here, all wrapped up." Lacing her fingers through his, she began to draw him over to the staircase.

He offered no resistance, only a question. "Where are we going?"

"Upstairs," she told him, leading the way. "I'd like to unwrap my present now."

"I never argue with a lady on Christmas Eve," Kullen deadpanned.

The smile that rose into Lilli's eyes when she looked at him over her shoulder made him fall in love with her all over again.

It was the fifth time that day.

* * * * *

COMING NEXT MONTH

Available December 28, 2010

#2089 A DADDY FOR JACOBY
Christyne Butler

#2090 FORTUNE'S PROPOSAL
Allison Leigh
The Fortunes of Texas: Lost...and Found

#2091 BEAUTY AND THE WOLF
Lois Faye Dyer
The Hunt for Cinderella

#2092 THE M.D. NEXT DOOR
Gina Wilkins
Doctors in the Family

#2093 MADE FOR A TEXAS MARRIAGE
Crystal Green
Billionaire Cowboys, Inc.

#2094 THE COWBOY CODE
Christine Wenger
Gold Buckle Cowboys

SPECIAL EDITION®

HARLEQUIN®

A Romance

FOR EVERY MOOD™

Spotlight on
Classic

Quintessential, modern love stories
that are romance at its finest.

See the next page
to enjoy a sneak peek from
the Harlequin Presents® series.

*Harlequin Presents® is thrilled
to introduce the first installment of
an epic tale of passion and drama by*
**USA TODAY *Bestselling Author
Penny Jordan!***

*When buttoned-up Giselle first meets
the devastatingly handsome Saul Parenti,
the heat between them is explosive....*

"LET ME GET THIS STRAIGHT. Are you actually suggesting
that I would stoop to that kind of game playing?"

Saul came out from behind his desk and walked toward
her. Giselle could smell his hot male scent and it was making
her dizzy, igniting a low, dull, pulsing ache that was taking
over her whole body.

Giselle defended her suspicions. "You don't want me here."

"No," Saul agreed, "I don't."

And then he did what he had sworn he would not do,
cursing himself beneath his breath as he reached for her,
pulling her fiercely into his arms and kissing her with all
the pent-up fury she had aroused in him from the moment
he had first seen her.

Giselle certainly *wanted* to resist him. But the hand she
raised to push him away developed a will of its own and
was sliding along his bare arm beneath the sleeve of his
shirt, and the body that should have been arching away
from him was instead melting into him.

Beneath the pressure of his kiss he could feel and taste
her gasp of undeniable response to him. He wanted to
devour her, take her and drive them both until they were
equally satiated—even whilst the anger within him that
she should make him feel that way roared and burned its

resentment of his need.

She was helpless, Giselle recognized, totally unable to withstand the storm lashing at her, able only to cling to the man who was the cause of it and pray that she would survive.

Somewhere else in the building a door banged. The sound exploded into the sensual tension that had enclosed them, driving them apart. Saul's chest was rising and falling as he fought for control; Giselle's whole body was trembling.

Without a word she turned and ran.

Find out what happens when Saul and Giselle succumb to their irresistible desire in

THE RELUCTANT SURRENDER

Available January 2011 from Harlequin Presents®

REQUEST YOUR FREE BOOKS!

2 FREE NOVELS PLUS 2 FREE GIFTS!

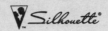

SPECIAL EDITION

Life, Love and Family!

YES! Please send me 2 FREE Silhouette® Special Edition® novels and my 2 FREE gifts (gifts are worth about $10). After receiving them, if I don't wish to receive any more books, I can return the shipping statement marked "cancel." If I don't cancel, I will receive 6 brand-new novels every month and be billed just $4.24 per book in the U.S. or $4.99 per book in Canada. That's a saving of 15% off the cover price! It's quite a bargain! Shipping and handling is just 50¢ per book.* I understand that accepting the 2 free books and gifts places me under no obligation to buy anything. I can always return a shipment and cancel at any time. Even if I never buy another book from Silhouette, the two free books and gifts are mine to keep forever.

235/335 SDN E5RG

Name	(PLEASE PRINT)	
Address		Apt. #
City	State/Prov.	Zip/Postal Code

Signature (if under 18, a parent or guardian must sign)

Mail to the Silhouette Reader Service:
IN U.S.A.: P.O. Box 1867, Buffalo, NY 14240-1867
IN CANADA: P.O. Box 609, Fort Erie, Ontario L2A 5X3

Not valid for current subscribers to Silhouette Special Edition books.

Want to try two free books from another line?
Call 1-800-873-8635 or visit www.morefreebooks.com.

* Terms and prices subject to change without notice. Prices do not include applicable taxes. N.Y. residents add applicable sales tax. Canadian residents will be charged applicable provincial taxes and GST. Offer not valid in Quebec. This offer is limited to one order per household. All orders subject to approval. Credit or debit balances in a customer's account(s) may be offset by any other outstanding balance owed by or to the customer. Please allow 4 to 6 weeks for delivery. Offer available while quantities last.

Your Privacy: Silhouette is committed to protecting your privacy. Our Privacy Policy is available online at www.eHarlequin.com or upon request from the Reader Service. From time to time we make our lists of customers available to reputable third parties who may have a product or service of interest to you. If you would prefer we not share your name and address, please check here. ☐

Help us get it right—We strive for accurate, respectful and relevant communications. To clarify or modify your communication preferences, visit us at www.ReaderService.com/consumerschoice.

SSE10R

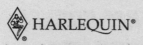

HARLEQUIN®

American ★ Romance®

C.C. COBURN
Colorado Cowboy

American Romance's
Men of the West

It had been fifteen years since Luke O'Malley,
divorced father of three, last saw his high school
sweetheart, Megan Montgomery. Luke is shocked to
discover they have a son, Cody, a rebellious teen on his
way to juvenile detention. The last thing either of them
expected was nuptials. Will these strangers rekindle
their love or is the past too far behind them?

**Available January
wherever books are sold.**

"LOVE, HOME & HAPPINESS"